T0286102

THE PRIDE LIST

EDITED BY SANDIP ROY AND BISHAN SAMADDAR

The Pride List presents works of queer literature to
the world. An eclectic collection of books of queer
stories, poems, plays, biographies, histories,
thoughts, ideas, experiences and explorations, the
Pride List does not focus on any specific region, nor
on any specific genre, but celebrates the great diversity
of LGBTQ+ lives across countries, languages,
centuries and identities, with the conviction that
queer pride comes from its unabashed expression.

The Worst Thing of All Is the Light

JOSÉ LUIS SERRANO

Translated from the Spanish
by Lawrence Schimel

LONDON NEW YORK CALCUTTA

ACCIÓN CULTURAL
ESPAÑOLA

Support for the translation of this book was
provided by Acción Cultural Española, AC/E

Seagull Books, 2023

First published in Spanish as *Lo peor de todo es la luz* by José Luis Serrano

Original Spanish text and images © José Luis Serrano, 2015

© Editorial EGALES, S.L. 2015

First published in English translation by Seagull Books, 2023

English translation © Lawrence Schimel, 2023

ISBN   978 1 80309 256 0

British Library Cataloguing-in-Publication Data

A catalogue record for this book is available from the British Library

Typeset at Seagull Books, Calcutta, India

Printed and bound by Hyam Enterprises, Calcutta, India

For Mikel, again

Had I the heavens' embroidered cloths,
Enwrought with golden and silver light,
The blue and the dim and the dark cloths
Of night and light and the half light,
I would spread the cloths under your feet:
But I, being poor, have only my dreams;
I have spread my dreams under your feet;
Tread softly because you tread on my dreams.

W. B. Yeats

Friday, 15 August 2014.
Alhóndiga

It had been raining all week, but our arrival in Bilbao coincided with a delicious afternoon of clear skies, air that was clean and salty, and cool temperatures. You busied yourself with family affairs while I took a walk through the Alhóndiga, converted into a cultural centre a few years ago. It was a holiday and few people were on the streets. Maybe the yearned-for but fleeting sunlight had led all of them to the beach, or they had taken advantage of the holiday weekend to flee the city. Only some youths (Moroccans or Algerians, perhaps) were seated in the shade with their mobiles, making use of the free wi-fi. I walked beneath the skylights that let one see the bottom of the indoor pool on the upper floor, which we'd never swum in despite my begging. From the first day, I'd been fascinated by the shadows of the swimmers on the ceiling, as if they were flying, or their feet and legs when they touched the bottom, suddenly pinkish and enormous on contact with the glass, when until then they had been nothing more than bluish figures who slid from one side to the other, tirelessly and at a relaxed pace, calm, one would say they were kites, a contest between aquatic and aerial kites. There are some families attending the underground cinema and groups of friends who now emerge from the three or four restaurants nearby (it's four in the afternoon). First I take a stroll around the plaza examining every corner, trying to compare it with my last visit now a year ago: the new bars that have opened, the restaurants that have changed owners or the kind of cuisine they serve. I remember the Loca de Arrikibar, that woman who sat on a bench in the plaza knitting, that is to say, *loca de amor*, waiting in front of the shop that belonged to the man she was in love with ('and the neighbourhood youth call her *loca*') every afternoon (the actress Lola Herrera took a photo as the Loca de Arrikibar and it is online everywhere, google it). I think there is a petition for the Bilbao Town Council to make a monument to her. A monument to love. (You know my obsession: what's important is to love, whether or not it's reciprocated. And the Loca loved a lot, she loved every afternoon, seated on her bench in the plaza, knitting children's socks—pink, blue, yellow and white—despite being called crazy so often.) I go and buy some liquorice from one of those shops that are open at all hours and I sit down on a bench next to the entrance to the cinema, like the Loca, in love (but you do love me back and I don't need to knit, except for these pages, if knitting and writing are alike in any way, which I think they are). I go back into the main hall again and wander beneath the projection of a gigantic sun. I've always imagined that there's a telescope pointing at the real sun and transmitting images in real time. Around the sun's black-and-orange corona, gigantic explosions blur the contours of the disk in dazzling flares. I like to look at the sun now that I can't

(I shouldn't) look at the real one. I try to go to the lavatory, but there is only one, and three or four men with baby carriages are waiting in queue. I guess they worry that there isn't a bathroom in the cinema and take advantage of this moment before entering. I think of Edorta and Koldo, I think of what they'd be doing now, if they wouldn't be in this very queue, one August Sunday, with their children, waiting for the film to begin. Wanting to be together even if only a while, an hour and a half or a little less, in silence and in the dark, smelling one another. One of the Moroccan youths approaches and asks me for a cigarette, but I don't smoke. And a joint? I smile. I ask him for the wi-fi password and he tells me it's open, no password needed. But that it's very slow. I see his friends are talking to the screen. They must all be on Skype talking perhaps with parents or siblings, there in Fez, or in Kenitra, or in El Jadida, or in Oran. Of course, how could it not be slow, I say, if you're all here using it. He laughs. A few of his teeth have already fallen out, despite his being so young. But he has a lovely smile, and those black eyes he shares with his friends.

I go up to the terrace. A few tables under umbrellas and lovely, unvarnished whitish flooring (I've seen it in many homes around here, it turns out quite elegant). There aren't a lot of people, but it's Friday afternoon on a holiday and one can see a certain relaxation in people's faces with the perspective of the entire weekend still ahead of them. They drink gin-tonics and mojitos and I'd very much like to drink one, whatever. But I resist the temptation and decide to wait for you, to see if I can convince you, despite your surely wanting to drink a café con leche at some bar in the Casco Viejo, the old part of town—in the kasko, as you all usually say, the way you write it. I peer through the railing to look at the front plaza, but I can only make out multicoloured awnings, traditional buildings squeezed between curved-glass office buildings, erected no doubt after the fever of the museums. The sky is so clear and there is not a single cloud now, although in the shade there is a slight breeze that would be inconceivable now in Madrid at this height of summer. I am always surprised when I see you pack your suitcase and add the sweaters, a jacket, even a polar fleece. I wear t-shirts from the end of May and still haven't interiorized that, as soon as we reach Bilbao, I'll appreciate long sleeves when night falls and even a blanket on the bed. I go back down the main hall. The Moroccan kid asks me if I know the mediateca. That word amuses me. I follow him and he leads me by lift to a lovely library in which, what's more, one can read the newspaper and even watch videos in a set of mini-rooms separated by plastic curtains, like the kind used in the doorways of Manchego towns so mosquitos don't get in. A small sofa and a small standing lamp: an atmosphere that aspires to be intimate to invite one to sit down and watch a movie and which, however, I think doesn't manage to pull it off—too much light, too many things that distract the attention, as if one sought not intimacy but exhibition. But now everything is like that. The kid shows it to me proudly, as if he were the one who'd thought of all this, as if he were the owner, the promoter, the architect. Through an interior window, I look at the area where there are small kids, and one of the parents who earlier waited in line for the bathroom now helps his son to draw what from a distance looks to me like a dog, a German Shepherd, but maybe not, it could be anything, I can't see it well, I don't see well. He could be Koldo. Koldo drew. Koldo would draw. Edorta is the one who would write. Edorta is the one who writes. But not now, now I write. I shall explain everything to all of you if you just have a little patience.

And you arrive. You give me a kiss. You smile sadly. You come from seeing your uncle at the old-age home.

'Everything OK?'

'As good as can be expected. Neither better nor worse. What have you been up to?'

'Strolling around here. I went up to the terrace, it's lovely. Do you want to go up?'

'Another time, I'd prefer to take a walk along the river to the kasko. As long as the sun is out . . .'

'Fine. Sounds good to me.'

'Have you kept going?'

'Of course, I've been wondering what Koldo and Edorta would be doing on a day like today, at this time. Perhaps they'd been eating here, or in one of the restaurants nearby. And then they'd gone up to have a gin-tonic on the terraza with the baby carriages in the shade.'

'Wow. They already have names? And children? I don't know why I thought they wouldn't both have Basque names. That they'd be like you and me.'

'Well no, I've decided that they're both Basque. Perhaps they were called by Spanish names at school, but not any longer. At home, they're always called like that. They're two lovely names, don't you think?'

'All Basque names are lovely.'

'Not all. But many, yes.'

'If we had children, we'd give them Basque names.'

'That's what you thought. They'd be named Tadeo and Sebastián. Did you ever meet the Loca de Arrikibar?'

'I don't know what you're talking about.'

We leave. On the street one can see a few groups of kids. The festivities begin tomorrow and perhaps they already can taste the week that awaits them. We approach the Guggenheim and go down the steps on the left side, towards the ría. There is a terraza nearby where I've thought to set a scene (perhaps the final scene) this very summer. A Sunday afternoon. It could be the summer of 24 August 2014. My holidays end on that day and I need that sensation to carry the final conversation between Koldo and Edorta to some desolate place, with no exit. For some reason, at least for me, I think endings that are devastating and with no exit leave more of a mark on the reader, on the viewer. Or not. I still don't know, I'm still not sure what to do. But the uncertainty makes the novel grow, makes it grow all by itself. That terraza, next to the museum, always full of families, of children, gives me the perfect point of supposed pleasure crossed by bleak monotony, in how what could be a marvellous afternoon turns into a jail, into a prison. But I don't know, as I said; I'd also like to leave them some hope, a certain future (even if a distant one) to hold on to. On the one hand, I'm tempted for one of the two families to suffer a tragedy. But I don't now if I would dare to write about it. I don't want to mislead readers. I want the tragedy to be the impossibility of their love. Or the impossibility of expressing, of materializing, their love, and its dissolution over time. But their love has not been impossible. Only difficult. And scarce. And inexpressible. I shall tell you.

'But that is the tragedy of all loves, no? That dissolution over time.'

'Yes, but one thing is for it to dissolve over time—all loves wind up in separation or in death, that's the sad fact—and another very different thing is that they never see it fulfilled and always retain the bigger sensation of having lost, of not having ever had anything, of having missed the train. Or of not having known to speak it. That it has been unspeakable.'

'And doesn't that happen to everyone?'

'I don't think so, to tell the truth. With you I don't have the sensation of not having always (or almost always) done (and said) everything. We've been together for twenty years. It's true that it would be ideal to carry on like this for all eternity, but, if this were to end tomorrow, I could only think of how happy we've been together, at least of how happy I've been. If I were to die right now, I could give thanks to whomever (I'd like to be able to thank God, Allah, Buddah, Jehovah—my thirst for Gods is not sated with just one, I can never get enough) for a full and happy life, I haven't wanted anything else, I don't want anything else. More time? Of course, all the time in the world. But there isn't. We don't know if there will be.'

You don't say anything, you don't even respond with a 'me too' which I would've appreciated. This is so very me, saying things. That's why I write. But you are a little like Koldo, although you don't paint. I keep talking.

'But for them, they couldn't have that sensation because they never even had the courage (I don't know if that is the word), the possibility of saying one to the other what they need, how good they are together, nor even of telling everyone, because they have nothing. Or that's what it seems to them, at least to Edorta: that they have nothing. Their love—joy for them—consists of spending more time together, in prolonging as much as possible those moments of closeness that are increasingly rare.'

'You've lost me now.'

'It's not easy, I don't know if I'll be able to pull it off. You and I have always talked about how important the quality of love is versus quantity. When you were away for work and we didn't see one another on weekends, we concentrated all our love in a few hours. They don't have that, can't have that. Their love is always the same (always absolute) and they can only enjoy it in time. They don't care about quality because the quality is always excellent, the best. They just need quantity, and that's what they don't have. And every day they have even less of it. They want to return to the schoolyard, to those never-ending recesses.'

'And our love isn't always absolute?'

'You're so cute sometimes!'

We continue walking along the ría, along the new pathway that makes Bilbao seem like some American city, so different from the city I first encountered in 1994, so distant from the city of Koldo and Edorta's childhood, from your own. That first time I arrived at night, and you led me to see the modernist facade of a cinema, or some theatre, that was half in ruins, or at least that's how I remember it, heavily buttressed with orange metallic beams. I must remind you to take me there again, if it still exists (I hope so). We pass under the Isozaki towers, which make me feel so relaxed. Those black prisms that reach towards the clouds, which pass along their shining facades like the swimmers in the Alhóndiga's ceiling. There must be something in Bilbao, in the ambience, that lifts us towards the sky, that wants to raise us to the heavens, the way tomato plants turn in search of the sun. Perhaps the nearby Iberdrola tower is the final manifestation of that yearning for light, for sky. Isozaki has understood this city perfectly although I'm sure all of you don't like it. You never like what knows you so well.

It's still a nice afternoon and the pathway is full of married couples with baby carriages, groups of young people, Nigerian men selling things: blue handkerchiefs for the fiestas, DVDs and CDs. We cross the Arenal bridge: the Arriaga theatre shines ochre with the afternoon's last sun, which no longer reaches the Casco Viejo, as dark as always. They're just finishing placing the txosnas and, at one of them, two twenty-something men joke and push and end up rolling on the ground, already drunk before time. What a week awaits them.

'That's what you're referring to, I suppose?'

'More or less. Unable to control their affective impulses, they usually start by a caress of hair or neck, a pat on the back or even the butt, sometimes kisses and bites, but soon they wind up fighting, as if they were ashamed.'

'As if they were? I think they are, which makes them pretend. So that no one thinks that they're . . .'

'Maricones,' I say, since it's not hard for me.

The guys have heard me say the word faggots and they get up from the ground. One of them approaches a blonde girl wandering around there (painting posters that lie on the ground, giving instructions to other girls) and he gives her a kiss on the neck, very affectionate, which she accepts delighted (and somewhat surprised). The other kid stares at us, wary and surly. For a moment it seems like he's going to say something to us, but we're two men near fifty, I with a beard, you unshaven. We're often confused for plainclothes cops: the Nigerians gather up their blankets of merchandise. When we enter some bar in the kasko, there are groups of men who suddenly stop talking; when we go to the towns of Vizcaya or

Guipúzcoa, it's not odd for us to be watched from behind some window, between the slats of the blinds. So the boy falls quiet and takes a drink from his plastic glass of kalimotxo.

We reach a cafeteria in the Casco Viejo that's been run by lesbians for decades now. It has an outdoor terraza, on a pedestrian street that ends at the ría. We order a café (you) and a beer (me—I never drink coffee because of palpitations) and we read the newspapers to see what the weather will be like tomorrow. The weather, always the weather. It calls to mind Blas de Otero.

Pristine Christine

(The Sea Urchins, Sarah Records, 001, 1987)

helping myself
for you is too hard I think
but leaving it inside
now that don't make me feel nice
everyone's turn now
you've hurt me

The worst thing of all is the light because it's always the same, but we are not ever the same, and then that light reminds us of the others we were before, once, those others who did things that now we wouldn't do, that we don't admit to having done. In spring, the light of a clear, bright day, when the wind has left the air clean and pure, leads us to clearer days, days of youth, of holidays. Or that yellow light of autumn, also clean, sharp at the final hours of the afternoon. The pure light of an August day without a single cloud (rare here, in the north, those clear days): at dawn; at midday, when the sea seems full of stars, which makes the sand sparkle like the firmament, all stars of those August days, the light of the infinite afternoon, of the twilight. The leaden light of muggy days on which it seems like time no longer flows but for the temperature rising around midday and some timid ray that doesn't manage to emerge, more a sensation than anything else that something glimmers beyond the clouds. The grey light of a winter day, days that are so short that it's said it wasn't daytime for even a moment. The brilliant light as well of some other days of winter, light frozen and radiant like a journey to the North Pole. The light of storms: the light before the lightning burst, the almost not-light when black clouds cover the sky, the light after rain, everything clean and washed. That light, as I say, is always the same, it repeats year after year, season after season, and every new nuance, every new tone, leads us to other moments whose sole nexus with who we are now is the light.

And so perhaps, after all, the light is a consolation, being at least the same, given that we almost never ever are, and if we want to be what we were at one moment, remember what we loved at one moment, forget perhaps for an instant that which we are now and what doesn't quite please us altogether, understand why we've become this, if we are to blame or not, the light is perhaps a guide, a shepherd, a lighthouse. Being the same light always, being that light repeated every autumn, the light of August that enters the room during the siesta through the half-closed blinds, drawing little squares on the white gotelé walls and making the dust, invisible until then, vibrate, the dust that we ourselves are, little bits of us that the light illuminates for brief moments before dying definitively (often I think that in that dust there are cells of mine that have not yet died, perfectly reproducible bits of myself that live, briefly, floating in the space around me), being, as I say, that same light always, I can close my eyes now, here, now alone, now that I don't see you, that we see one another so little, now that we have nothing left.

The light of the schoolyard where we met one now-distant afternoon, the light of the locker room, especially in autumn, when daylight saving ends, and now as early as four, and if it's cloudy outside, the lights need to be turned on because through the frosted glass only a weak greyish light slips in from the street, the light of November, when night falls very quickly, and then it is an orange light, the light of the street-lamps, but not a light that evokes oranges or mandarins—the light of hospitals, of industrial estates, of ring roads, the light of the street where you live, the light of the cars parked haphazardly, double or triple parked, in front of the bakery, the light of the bakery itself, the light of London one August of 1992 (or was it in 1989? Is it possible that I need to look it up, that I don't recall the exact date?), the light of Underground entrances and exits, the light of Holland Park, perhaps the worst of them all (because that afternoon I knew we'd arrived there, that this was happiness, but that there wouldn't be any more of it, and that it had ended), the light cast by a line of shrubs, with a gentle, broken shadow on your face, as if the little leaves caressed your skin and the golden glimmer of the sun in your eyes vibrated to thank them, the light of the Barinatxe beach, at sunset, when I'm trying to tell you, trying to explain something that even I don't understand, which I don't know if anyone shall ever understand, the light of an alleyway in your neighbourhood some December afternoon (but it's already night), the light of a terraza next to the Guggenheim on an August afternoon at the end of the summer when the holidays are ending and it's Sunday and the marvellous afternoon becomes a jail or a prison, the light of when we're not together, the orange light of the streetlamps and the light of bottlenecked cars, red, white, long lights that dazzle; that illuminate your face briefly, just at that moment when you say goodbye, brushing the back of my neck with a slight caress of your fingers, so slight that the touch doesn't actually happen and, yet, your heat remains there all night; that briefly illuminates your half smile, yearning, which also awaits, which needs, some touch from me. I usually give you a little tickle above your hip, that nameless place that's so vulnerable and thin (at least, I don't know its name, I don't know if I've ever known it and, if I once did, I don't remember it), and then you laugh. You laughed. Not now, of course, now that we no longer laugh. And if we do, if we laugh, it's so as not to cry. But we've cried little, you and I. Together, I mean. I can't be sure about on our own in your case, but as for me . . . I have indeed cried a lot and still do while I write (and I'll weep even more when I finish doing so and then, perhaps, I shall finally stop crying, at least for this, for you). But not that afternoon: you laughed.

'See you tomorrow, Edorta.'

'See you tomorrow, Koldo.'

I write: 'I am not myself. It is one of those afternoons when I am not myself. I am an old man who loses himself down foggy paths, wearing chequered slippers stained with mud,

I spit with every step, and I stop to pee something greenish and cold, something that is not mine, which I can't imagine how it comes out of me, I piss myself on my grey leg, the mist and saliva freezes, I step on some cowshit and softly mumble a meaningless Our Father, always repeating the same phrase, forgive us our trespasses, forgive us our trespasses, lead us not into temptation and, if you do, forgive us our trespasses.'

Saturday, 16 August 2014.
Castro Urdiales

The sky dawned very dark and the forecast in the papers presaged a lousy day. So we decided to take a stroll through Castro Urdiales. The bus left us near the main plaza and right away we went down to the boardwalk (I always have an urgent need to see the sea if I'm nearby). A greyish light didn't block these timid rays from arising on the horizon, which gently illuminated what seemed from the distance to be heavy downpours. The waves broke into foam on crashing against the pier.

'Look, little sheep,' you said, recalling a girl we met in Malta who always spoke in pastoral terms to refer to rough seas.

'It's full of little sheep. Like how it always was in Malta.'

We decide to first approach the rocky promontory that separates the beaches from the city to try and visit the lighthouse, to walk a bit out to the breakwater, the church, and a temporary painting exhibition. As we pass through the fishing port, a group of children launch their rod into the dark sea, there below, in what seemed a competition for tourists on a day of bad weather (that's the good thing about the North: there are always options when there's bad weather, there's bad weather often, it's all been thought out). Beside the port, burly youths entered and emerged from the wharves with the traineras. I always wound up spellbound watching their activities.

'This is where Koldo will come to train.'

'So far? He's come from Bilbao to Castro to row?'

'His mother will bring him (she's a widow). By car, until he's fourteen, and then he'll keep coming on his own by bus until he's eighteen. It's just that I think I'm going to kill off the mother as well. Then he'll give it up while he's at university (I still haven't decided what he'll study) but he'll keep rowing sporadically with friends.'

'Wouldn't it be more logical for it to be Zierbena, which is closer?'

'It's been forever since we went to Ciérvana. We'd have to go so I could have a better idea of what it's like. If we go one of these days, I'll change it. Otherwise, I'll keep Castro.'

'Castro will be strange. But everything will be strange . . . '

'You're such a comedian.'

I stop to listen to the young men, and their shouts shimmer and echo through the port as if it were covered by a steel bell.

'Don't you realize that all these boys speak Euskera? They're from Vizcaya. From Bilbao, I'm sure. As if we were there.'

'Whatever you say. But it didn't used to be so easy to get to Castro like it is now.'

'Mothers will do anything for their children. Koldo's, what's more, is a Mother Courage. She'll be a Mother Courage. She was a Mother Courage.'

We walked along the pier to the tip that reached out into the ocean. I breathed deeply to fill my lungs with salt and water. On the way back from our stroll, we went to the exhibition hall in which a local painter, now elderly, was presenting his canvases (of sailors, fishermen, saints) with obvious (and logical, since this was classical in art) satisfaction and open delight in male bodies. The girl in charge of the exhibition hall told us that he was a famous painter, that he was around if we wanted to talk to him, that in some of the churches of the city centre he had painted altarpieces, or frescos, years ago. There were photos of the altarpieces.

'And now you're getting into homoeroticism in painting?'

'But, don't you realize? I'm not talking about sexual desire, but admiration for the beauty of the male body. That happens.'

'Is that what happens to Edorta with Koldo's body?'

'And vice versa?'

'And it's not sexual?'

'I don't think so. If it were sexual, they'd fuck at some point. The nights are very long and there are a lot of them. I think that whoever wants to do something winds up doing it if the opportunity presents itself, and these two are going to have (had) a lot of opportunities.'

'And they don't do it. They didn't do it. They won't do it.'

'You're starting to talk like me. No, of course they don't. That's what all this is, that's what this is all about. In any case, why do we give so much importance to fucking, which to me, personally, seems like a frivolity, like standing on your head, like doing cartwheels, like touching the tip of your nose with your tongue? Can you imagine if we'd created a social identity around people able to touch the tip of their nose with their tongues, and these people would be associated with—I don't know—the enjoyment of eating standing up at the bar, the pleasure of giving a tip to the usher at the cinema, they'd be considered good at plasterwork, they'd crowd electronic music concerts?'

'You're getting all tangled up now.'

You fall silent and glare at me. We go up to the lighthouse. I always wanted to be a lighthouse keeper, but unfortunately there are fewer than ever because the lighthouses are operated mechanically now. On the horizon, the sun begins to shine from behind the clouds and the light filters through the curtains of dark water, like in a provincial living room in the 80s when we fled from the light with always-closed thick curtains. The waves keep battering the breaker, but not too violently. We'd seen photos of the storms from the previous winter in which it seemed the sea would wind up swallowing everything. We go up to a terraza in front of the main door of the lighthouse, which you can't climb up, at least not today (I'm out of luck). It has a lovely view of the Roman bridge (which is medieval), the hermitage of Santa Ana and Santa María de la Asunción, which we decide to practically run to visit because we've been told it's about to close. Inside the church (a Gothic one from the early eighteenth century) we're invaded by a vague subaquatic clarity, with that strange luminous reverberation that churches near the ocean have. A young man greets us as we pass and, somewhat bored, tells us that, if we have any questions, he's there for what we want. An excursion of elderly Russians, whom we had gotten ahead of on the access stairs, enters shouting and we decide that the magic is over. The young man looks at us with disgust and raises his eyes to the roof of the nave, the painted sky, asking who knows what. I also have implored, I always ask for things in churches and I always give thanks beforehand. But I do know what I'm asking for and why I'm giving thanks.

We decide to continue along the sea on our way to the Ostende beach. I was determined to reach the cemetery. I had an image from the film *El abuelo* stuck in my head and I've always associated it with Castro Urdiales without ever being too sure, how these ideas get into your head without knowing very well why, or their reliability. We cross through a neighbourhood of four-storey homes ('cheap houses' they were called in the 80s), a neighbourhood of workmen and sailors, I suppose, with laundry hung from the windows drying in the marine breeze. I've always found such ugly houses curious, with their peeling grey-brown rendering, beside the sea. And I've seen them in lots of places: in Venice, in La Valeta, in Cadiz. It's as if, because they're cheap, they were made on purpose against the sea rather than in its favour, ignoring it, ashamed. The dark, narrow streets seem distant from the bluish splendour and I've always imagined the enormous difference (in mood, psychological) that living on the ground floor or first floor must entail—so far from the sea that as if it were almost a neighbourhood on the outskirts of Madrid, where the domestic smells condense (of chickpeas, cauliflower, socks, bleach, garbage)—in contrast to the glorious vista from the third or fourth floor, in whose rooms the sea slips in through the window and smells of salt and sand. I imagined its inhabitants to be different, those up above so far from those in the basement, so different. We cross a cove of smooth, round stones where the waves enter through a hole in the rock. The stones glimmer polychrome in the sunlight, which has suddenly emerged and begins to heat the air and make the water shine. I go down some steps to touch it, to plunge my hands and feet in the transparent water, clean and salty. I think once more of Edorta and Koldo, of how I am going to do this, of how I even dare to try to make understandable something I myself don't understand, which I'm not even sure exists (although something tells me that yes, it does exist, and that someone will understand me), I relish in the anticipated failure of not knowing how to do it, of not knowing how to explain it. Perhaps my task is just to tell it, to write it, without understanding and without judging. Perhaps my task is just that of failing. Not in vain, my two previous novels were nothing more than testimonies of my failure to try and tell a story, to try and write a novel.

It's nearing midday and the Ostende beach begins to fill with bathers who take advantage of the unexpected sunny afternoon. We've seen some restaurants near the shore, but it's still early for lunch and we decide to keep walking down the path that starts at the end of the beach and leads to the cemetery that I had such an urge to see, to assure myself that it did match that scene from *El abuelo* which I wasn't sure was real or imagined (this happens to me a lot). An enjoyable stroll during which one feels more on the Mediterranean than the Cantabrian, at least on this sunny midday with the water a pure blue, almost cobalt, and delicate at the same time, and the fragrant colourful grasses that poke between the stones. There are young men bathing in the small coves, to which one gains access (risking one's life) via steep promontories over the sea or they leap from the cliffs into the blue water. But surely the effort is worthwhile and from above it seems almost as if the freshness of the calmed water caresses us as well. A very handsome boy with a dog reads and sunbathes in the middle of a meadow.

'Koldo? Edorta?'

'Edorta. Koldo reads less. But he is more of an exhibitionist. So maybe yes, perhaps it's Koldo after all. Probably he isn't reading, it's just a pose. Typical of Koldo.'

'Well, to me he looks very focused. I'd kill to know what he's reading.'

'Not Proust, I can assure you.'

'Who knows?'

The boy looks up from his book, smiles at us, and waves. Pleased, I return the greeting. We reach the cemetery, which has a lovely view of the Cantabrian coast and which, however, bears no relation to the image I was looking for, but I don't care. We began to feel hungry and decide to return towards the Ostende beach before the restaurants fill up. We choose a small one with wooden tables in the street under the shade of some porticoes, facing the sea. The Russian waitress recommends the marmitako and the fried chicharro, to which we enthusiastically agree. We order wine and gaseosa and, after a good while resting in the shade, slightly drunk (especially me, I never leave a bottle of wine half-drunk if I don't have to work later), we set off towards the other beaches, towards the east.

It starts to get hot and everything points to Sunday going to be a perfect day to spend on the beach. We walk towards the Punta Cotolino and beneath the trees until we reach a chiringuito that's not too crowded at this time, overlooking the sea. I order an ice cream.

'But then, aren't you going to write a normal novel?'

'I never write a normal novel. What's more, I've always made it very clear that I'm unable to tell a story. There will just be snippets, bits of what could have been the novel. Perhaps a diary by Edorta.'

'And these dialogues.'

'That's right. Perhaps not these, but others I make up based on these.'

'And will I be myself? I'm worried about being myself in your novel, worried that you'll put me in your novel.'

'No, of course not. You won't be you. You'll be someone who dialogues with me, perhaps me dialoguing with myself to clarify things. And me asking myself or answering things, putting words in your mouth. If you don't mind, of course. But you won't mind because you won't be you.'

'Isn't it a bit complicated, artificially complicated?'

'Complicated, yes. But not artificially, I think. The world is complicated. Naturally complicated. Look at what happens to the phone cable when you leave it alone.'

'But it's going to be a novel about the love between two men?'

'That's right.'

'And they're not homosexuals.'

'Exactly.'

'Neither of them.'

'They're not even closeted.'

'And they won't be in the future?'

'No. They aren't and they won't be.'

'And they love one another.'

'Very much. Very very much.'

'And they don't desire one another sexually?'

'No, of course not.'

'You're sure?'

'Absolutely sure.'

'It's going to be hard work for you to explain it.'

'I know, but for them, too. For them everything is a lot of work, too.'

'Then you'll alternate chapters: our dialogues (or the dialogues with yourself) and Edorta's diary. In different-coloured ink?'

'I don't think that will be necessary. Our dialogues will take place over the course of ten days, during our summer holidays in Bilbao—August 2014, from the 15th to the 24th, specifically—in the real places where the novelized story of Koldo and Edorta takes place, which will last almost fifty years, from the time they're born in 1967 until that same summer of 2014.'

'They were born the same year as you?'

'It's easier for me. I didn't know Bilbao until 1994. If I need to speak of them from before that date, I need to use my own memories. In the end, I don't think Zorrotza in Bilbao, or Alcobendas in Madrid, were very different.'

'Well, there were a few distinctions.'

You fall silent and I know what you're thinking. I've grown used to understanding your silences ever since I came here the first time. You keep talking.

'Getting back to the subject. Are you planning to talk about all of that stuff you're always talking about, about the social construction of gender and how social conventions strangle both men as well as . . . ?'

I interrupt you. I'd like to explain to you now that I also think that not only is gender a social construct but sexual orientation as well. But let's take things slowly.

'And how feminism has managed little by little to make women see that, in effect, they are nothing more than conventions, but still hasn't managed to convince men that they are also victims of other constructions that oppress them (to a much lesser degree, needless to say, and with consequences that are much less grave, if we're talking of violence, of murders), especially in everything that has to do with feelings, their management, their manifestation and repression. As I said: not at all comparable to the situation of women, that's clear. But uncomfortable. And that can create unhappiness. It doesn't kill them, but some die of grief.'

'All of that you're going to talk about?'

'I'm going to try. Through Edorta's diaries. But I want those diaries to be interrupted, just fragments. For lots of time to pass between different scenes. As if the guy had decided to make some pages disappear, or as if there were no need to write for years. Above all I want the important things to not be in the diary, for them to remain elided. For it to be the reader who imagines what has happened between one date and another.'

'I repeat: isn't this all too complicated?'

'Let me say now that the way you know a person (and now it's the mathematician in me speaking) is discretely, never continuously. We have an idea of how other people are through our direct experience at specific moments in time, but we are not observing them twenty-four-seven. If that were the case, we could only ever watch one person without any rest. It's like that Borges map, which is as large as the territory itself it's said to represent. So we interpret in a discrete way, through little moments over time, the vicissitudes of the people around us. As we think best, as we want, as it fits us, almost always in a very prejudiced way because that's very easy, and without knowing everything because that's impossible. That will happen in the novel. Discrete moments frozen in time and empty spaces (of years) between those moments.'

'Crazy. You're crazy. Shall we go back?'

Emma's House

(The Field Mice, Sarah Records 012, 1988)

early morning by the harbour
the clouds above form one sheet that's grey
[...]
you have nothing to live up to
you have nothing to live down

The worst thing of all is the light of the schoolyard where we met one now-long-ago afternoon. I don't know why we were alone, the two of us, maybe punished, or we'd stayed an hour extra after lunch waiting for our parents to come pick us up. Your mother. My parents. Maybe—who knows?—they'd simply let us out into the yard to play (I remember the weather was great), and the yard was very large and we so little. The rest of the kids were on the other side, with the rectangular building in the middle of the elliptical yard. We decided to play a football match, just you and I. But we didn't want to play one against one: almost from the first moment we had decided that we were a team, that we were on the same side. Besides, we didn't have a ball. Suddenly the sky clouded over. That happens here a lot. Suddenly black clouds appear on the horizon on an afternoon of shining blue light and, in the shade, a cold breeze that gets into the bones reminds us that summer is over, that it's gone. You said that the spectators (there never were any, but you always imagined that you were the centre of attention of thousands of people, perhaps you felt that you always would be) would be cold and that they won't stay to watch us play. So we discovered a fantastic way to heat up the spectators: that area of the yard was sand. Dragging our feet, kicking sand into the air, everything filled with light orangish dust, a sort of cloud that you associated with heat, with the smoke of a bonfire. We were heating up the spectators for more than half an hour and the dust cloud was so large that we wound up covered in dust like two construction workers. We heard a teacher shouting from a window and we stopped raising the dust cloud. You laughed so hard when you saw my black hair (which was now blond) that you fell on your butt on the ground. At that moment I knew we would be friends. I felt perhaps that that afternoon would join us (fatally) forever. I wanted that match we still hadn't begun to play to go on eternally, as I still always want to prolong any moment when I am with you, when we are together and alone, to freeze it, even knowing that can't be done. I know that now. But I do imagine that afternoon as eternal, or they are many afternoons I mix together, and we win that game we play without a ball and against a non-existent team before invisible spectators who were no longer cold. You were the goalie and started with a huge kick that reached further than halfway down the field and I caught it with my chest and kicked it to you, because now you were the forward, but you didn't go for the goal and instead graciously sent it back to me so that I was the one who scored (as I had earlier done for you), or perhaps so the ref didn't whistle offside, something that neither you nor I understood very well, and you narrated each play shout by shout like the best Argentine sportscaster, and gave us the names of Athletic Club players from the time (Iribar, Uriarte, Zubiaga). Often we wound up rolling on the ground (our mothers would become fed up with sewing those knee pads and elbow pads that were used back then—from oilcloth, from plastic—onto our uniforms). You told me that your name was Koldo (but that perhaps in class they called you Luis—although they say that your father called you Koldobika and I, sometimes, to tease you, now call you Clodoveo). I told you that my name was Edorta, despite always being called Eduardo at home, or Eduardito. You have always called me Edorta since then.

One of those afternoons, leaving school, I met your mother, already a widow. So young and a widow, with three kids. You were the littlest, the one who had known your father the least. You didn't even remember him. He had died when you were two years old and you only felt a vague sensation in dreams, a slight memory of someone warm who smelled of tobacco, coffee, and apples who tossed you into the air. And you gave him the face, in your daydreams, of the man they said was your father in the (scant) photos in the family album. But you were your father, your aunts from Getxo said, you were just like your father, you're going to be the spitting image of him, the same square jaw, the same strong shoulders, the same height (they supposed because of your gigantic hands), the same square nose from the paintings by the Zubiaurres, by Aurelio Arteta. The other two brothers, already somewhat older, two little men, were already big, but you, you had to receive all the affection you needed, so little, so orphaned. I never found in your mother a single hint of self-pity. Not even a single tear, not even once a mistiness in her eyes after some commentary, after some disagreeable or tactless question. A strong woman, devoted to her sons, working in the accounting department of a mattress factory from eight until five and the rest of the afternoon collecting the boys from school and bringing them to Castro a few times a week to train in the port: all three of you boys liked the traineras, just like your deceased father, who'd won some minor trophies (as the living room of your home bore witness). Your mother there, at the door of the school, under an umbrella, with her hair always trimmed like a boy's (I'm sure she never had time to even dry it and that was the reason behind her decision, which caused comments among her girlfriends—*honey, you're never going to get married again like that*—long hair is such a bother and, besides, in this city nothing ever dries). Often you remained behind, the last ones, because she didn't arrive, and I watched you from behind, holding my mother's hand, or my father's, they took turns to bring me home, or to English class, or piano class, I was an only child, their only son, their treasure, their life (sometimes it's not good to put all your eggs in a single basket, my father said fearfully. I didn't know what he was talking about. My mother said that it didn't matter, that in this case, when it came to children, any broken egg was all of them). I looked back and there you three were—who knew what you talked about, seated under the porch because it always rained on those afternoons when your mother didn't arrive, some last-minute supplier wanting to be paid, some lost invoice, some frenetic boss who didn't understand that employees had private lives, or that there are always traffic jams when it rains, those narrow streets, all the cars on the road at the same time just then, cars double and triple parked, the windshield wipers that scratch and never quite clear everything and whine because the rubber is half worn and there is never time to change it, never time for anything.

I got home and told my mother that I had a little friend, who at first I called Luis, in case they weren't happy about his being Koldo, but my father started to joke with Koldobika-Clodoveo and after that at my home you were always Koldo or Clodo and never Luis. I went to bed happy wishing for the next day to dawn. We were now seated together in class, I don't know who decided it or when, surely some teacher who saw that we worked better together, that the benefit was mutual, and weekends seemed eternal to me, anxiously waiting for Monday to see you with your cheeks red from the cold, or from the way you three boys had to run so as not to arrive late from the corner where your mother had dropped you off so she didn't arrive late either. Sometimes, you didn't take off the little black jacket that I liked so much until a half hour had gone by, you told the teacher you were very cold. You had the cold in your bones, big boy, the teacher said, it was hot inside the classroom, you'll sweat, you'll get sick. But it was always the same and you spent the first half hour chattering until you warmed up. When I saw your house, years later, I understood about the cold, that it was something psychological, related to darkness and damp more than anything else. We went out into the yard and played football, with or without a ball, but always with invisible spectators, first warming up those spectators who had been infected with that perpetual cold, you shouting out every play with that voice that sometimes sounded Argentine, sometimes Mexican, sometimes Madrileño, and you gave us the names of players of the Athletic (Iribar, Uriarte, Zubiaga), and we threw ourselves to the ground and hugged every time we scored a goal (with or without a ball). Since then I've had (we've had, I think) the need to hug you (to hug one another, I think) like on those afternoons, although we've been able to do it very little. And that need kept growing bigger because of that scarceness, that inhibition. How hard Sundays were without your embrace. Sundays above all.

The worst thing of all is the light of Sundays in the afternoon because it's the most enjoyable moment, but only for those around me: people—the whole world—seem to enjoy an afternoon of glorious light, of good weather, and I, what I want is for it to be over, for it to be over already. Then my heart starts to ache and I want time to pass. For it to be night.

Sometimes, so many times, I'd like to go back to those school afternoons. To give you a shock, from behind, tickling you, mussing your hair, pulling your ears, giving you a nip on the neck, a pinch on your elbow, on that bit of flesh I always say you need to lose, to give you a slap on the head, on the neck, to squeeze your balls (there was a time, perhaps in the seventh year of school, when we all squeezed one another's nuts as a joke, as a greeting), to climb on your back, to race you, to trip you, to jump the steps of your home from landing to landing, wildly, to go to the funfair and ride with you on Octopus and raise my arms and grab you to me when I almost fall, to make you lose your balance if you're walking on the edge or on top of some fence, tugging your pants down, hugging you whenever the Athletic scored a goal, throwing ourselves on the ground and rolling over, giving you a nip on your dick like professional football players do, grabbing your butt, tugging the hairs on the nape of your neck, pissing into the window beside you, jerking off together, trying to see who could come first, who could come farther.

My Luis, my Koldo, my Clodo, so far away now, so far that I'm losing sight of you. That I no longer see you.

I write: 'Only the void, to think that not even death is a compensation, that it is a lie, that it does not await us like a treasure among the chests in the basement, but that everything is false, that we shall always remain here with the same miseries, with the eternal fears, of what? of eternity, of mud, of leaving a memory, of doing hurt to someone, of doing good to someone and their feeling obliged to thank you, of leaving traces, of another unending afternoon of sunshine, of summers, of December, of April, oh God! couldn't you at least skip some April?'

Sunday, 17 August 2014.
Beach

On Sunday we went to Barinatxe, our beach, where we've spent so many moments of happiness over the past twenty years. It's a broad beach at the foot of the Larrabasterra cliffs. The stones that fall loose form triangular heaps of rocks in the corners and the sand gathers against the cliffs in dunes covered with these very fragile little green plants that ecologists are always struggling to protect (the protected area expands each year and is now so vast that soon it's the bathers who will need to be protected). When the tide goes out, it's around 800 metres long to walk from one end of the beach to the other. It's usually full of surfers (Australian, French, German, Dutch, Belgian, Andalusian, Basque) because the waves are both high and long. There are no buildings nearby and, because of the steep access (which is not complicated, but going back uphill along the steps or ramp becomes a chore), the ambience is rather youthful and not as family-oriented as the beach next door. People practise nudism, although less each year, as if for some reason it were losing ground, or as if it had once been much more modern but not any longer. I love the Cantabrian Sea, I like the chilly water, the colder the better, and what I like most is to go in and out of the water. To heat up under the sun and then freeze in the water, and so on forever. You, however, hate it, and once you're in the water, you're able to hold out up to half an hour so as not to have to go in and out like I do. There's a little chiringuito that serves sandwiches and salads, soft drinks, beers, and ice cream (I seem to remember that years ago there were even two places) although on cloudy days it doesn't even open.

Above, where the car park is and the area from where people go hang-gliding, there are a few bars that we've got to know over the years, some of them even with a pretty decent but inexpensive menu, whose chefs are kids who study at high-end cooking schools and do their summer internships there. When you come out of the water, we usually take a stroll along the shore. And we talk, we talk lots, we've talked so much on that beach. I'd even say that my two earlier novels took shape during those delicious strolls along the shore. I play at walking a little behind you, to step in your footsteps. I once wrote a poem about that: 'The Footprints of Laetoli'. In Laetoli, an archaeological site in Tanzania dating from the lower Palaeolithic, the footprints of three hominids were found, one of which walked upon the prints of one of the others. They were calm, out strolling, like us today. So distant and so different. I've always thought of that hominid in Laetoli, why he would walk upon the footprints of his companion. Perhaps the ground was burning. Perhaps they only played. I'm sure that was it. A long time ago now, on one of the first trips I took with you, I played at closing my eyes when we walked back to the hotel along a long passageway with palm trees. After thirty steps one feels the vertigo of the void, a devastating uneasiness, one's steps start to wobble. Every night further, walking further with my eyes closed every night. You didn't even speak (what could you have been thinking about all that). The thing is that I continued, every night a little further, knowing that you were by my side and would warn me if I went astray. Today I've remembered that. I've always liked to fool around when I'm out walking with you.

'Nor do I want the diaries to be written on the specific date being talked about in them, I don't feel like recreating how an eight-year-old boy writes, a sixteen-year-old, a twenty-five-year-old, a man of forty. Perhaps it'll be a diary written retrospectively. More memoirs than a diary.'

'I don't know if I understand you.'

'Maybe Edorta's diary won't be exactly a diary. Maybe he carries a diary in his head, or he recounts things about his childhood when he's already thirty-three. It would be a kind of novelized diary, the transformation into a novel of a possible real diary. Perhaps the diary originates, complete, from the same date, from this self-same 2014. But it would also have bits written in poetic prose, a diary of feelings, a diary of what can't be said. Of what is only felt.'

'And how are you going to recreate Edorta's story, how are you going to get into his head? You're a homosexual, you're not going to understand him.'

'Homosexual? You're referring to the fact that sexual orientation being a social construction and an instrument of control (as I believe it is), I've decided to adopt as my own that category that they say defines me, despite my thinking that the only thing it defines are my sexual practices and never myself as a subject, but how (as I said) I've decided to accept as a political tool of visibilization and of struggle while people in the world exist who are stigmatized for those sexual practices? Why do we give more importance, all the importance, to fucking instead of touching the tip of the nose with our tongues? If I could touch my nose with my tongue, would I be a "nose-toucher"? Would people beat me, would I be killed for that?'

'You get off on this verbal masturbation. You think too much. And you sound like some queer theory manual.'

'It is my disgrace, to think and read. But, for your satisfaction, I do it less and less because each time I understand less. When someone tells me "I understand everything clearly" right away, I mistrust—surely what's going on is that they don't understand anything at all. Ignorance, which is quite bold. Once I went to protest about a geometry exam on which I'd got a one—such was my ignorance that I wasn't even aware of it. And that's the worst. When you don't even know that you don't know.'

I crouch down to grab an iridescent shell the tide has carried. The tides are very strong here, the beach advances and retreats hundreds of metres over the course of the day: sometimes we wind up altogether on a narrow strip. At others, we're spread out across the sand as far away from one another as it's possible to be.

'In answer to your question: I don't understand it. But I want to understand it. Perhaps this whole book is nothing more than the attempt (which might be a failed attempt, as always happens to me, but I learn something along the way) of understanding something that is painful for me. Deep down, what I am trying to do is to stop worrying about the people who surround me for what I think (or at least thought before I started writing) would have made them happier some other way. That is to say, I understand that they don't want more than what they have, and that if they have not come to have what you and I have, it's because they haven't wanted to, not from fear nor shame. But, on the other hand, I want it to be clear. I want to make it obvious that they suffer, that nobody accepts what they have either, that no one understands what happens to them, which—deep down—has no solution, because they want to have it all, always, together, but they can't. That it winds up dissipating, it winds up ending. They have girlfriends, kids, and every day they have less time and the one thing they want, the only thing they want, is time to be together.'

Days at the beach unfold deliciously slowly, but by not doing anything, when the sun is already very low on the horizon, one is aware of time passing almost suddenly, and the strange sensation that the day has gone by too quickly. We gather up our scattered clothing and return to rest for a bit, to eat a bit, to grab our jackets before going out.

At night we went to Bilbao to see the fireworks. We usually take a train from a stop near your father's house that leaves us, in ten minutes, at the central station, in Abando. We go down towards the ría, among the crowds, which already clump into any place, waiting for the fireworks to begin. We almost always find a place near the Town Council, on the Ripa pier, although sometimes we've gone up to Extebarria Park, where there are the cachivaches of the feria, the tombolas, the food areas serving bocadillos and fried chicken. At those hours, and despite the heat of the day, it's almost always cool. Almost everyone wears jackets or cardigans, even if just tied around their waists or necks: the night is long and it will get colder and damper, especially towards dawn. Beside us, young couples weighed down with buggies eat sandwiches and drink beer unconcerned, happily. Two men pass by, drunk, one with his arm on the other's shoulder. From the mountain the first rocket is launched: it's a warning, soon things are going to start.

'Are your boys going to watch the fireworks?'

'I suppose so, of course. Doesn't everyone?'

'Well, not everyone. Bilbao is very big, there are lots of places from where you can't even hear them. Although the lights, yes, one can see the lights from everywhere.'

'It's a strange moment, isn't it? This business of the fireworks. How it brings us together. Like eating grapes on New Year's. Everyone doing the same thing at the same time.'

'As I said, not everyone does watch it.'

'But it has to do in some way with Bilbao identity. No? If it isn't the epitome of Bilbao identity. Like the Isozaki towers (but that's what I think).'

'I don't know. You're simplifying. When I was little, I didn't watch them. What's more: I think there weren't even festivities. At least, not like this. I don't think it can be the definition of Bilbao identity, because it seems to me that Bilbao identity existed long before fireworks did.'

'Yes, of course. Back to the Neolithic. In any event, you are from Bilbao, but not from the centre.'

All the lights have been turned off and the music from the txosnas has stopped resounding.

Zas, puuuum, fiiiiiuuuuuuuuuuuuuuu, tat-tat-tat-tat-tat. Prrrrrtttttt. Puuuuum. Ooooohhhhhhhhh.

'Give me your hand.'

'I can't hear you, I don't know what you're saying.'

'I said give me your hand. Don't be like Koldo.'

Zas, puuuum, fiiiiiuuuuuuuuuuuu, tat-tat-tat. Prrrtttt.

Puuuuum. Oooooohhhhhhhhh. Zas, puuuuum, fiiiuuuuuu, tat-tat-tat-tat-tat. Prrrrrtttttttt. Puuuuuum. Oooooohhhhhhhh. Zas, puuum, fiiiiiuuuuuuuuuuuu, tat-tat-tat. Prrrtttt. Puuuuum. Oooooohhhhhhhhh.

The Centre of My Little World

(Another Sunny Day, Sarah Records 613, 1992)

when I saw you getting off the bus
I knew this whole wide world was made for us
and the first time that I spoke to you,
I was so shy I didn't know what to do

The worst thing of all is the light of November because night falls very quickly, and then it's an orange light, a sodium light, from the street lamps. But it's not a light that evokes oranges or mandarins: it's a light of hospitals, of industrial estates, of ring roads. Your mother had already passed away, the summer before. The first three months passed when I almost never saw you. Three orphaned kids, so small (well, only you were little. Or almost). Weeks of decisions as to what was best. My mother even spoke of you coming to live with us (nothing would have pleased me more, of course). But in the end, an aunt of yours, single, a sister of your mother's, went to live in your home—delighted and happy, people said, because she had found a meaning for her life. And among the two families of the deceased they took care that you should lack for nothing, or at least, that you lacked the same things as before. Ever since your mother died I felt that if no one loved you any more in this world, at least no one as she had loved you, she who thought constantly of you (of all of you, but mostly of you, who were the littlest), which was the first thing she did when she woke up and the last thing she did when she went to bed, at least I should begin to love you in that way so you didn't feel alone. Or, if it wasn't in that way, in a similar way. Although I already thought that I loved you in my way, and that that way was also legitimate. And enormous.

It was still earlier, we still had at least half an hour. Of course, for you, now they no longer gave you time limits. They're going to lose control, my mother said, a desmadrarse. They are already desmadrados, and also des-padrados, my father said, it's strange that the word despadrar doesn't exist, as if the kids wouldn't go wild as well with the lack of the father, or who knows, maybe even without missing either of the two (and he looked at me, as if I might already be desmadrando or despadrando through contagion). They let me stay out until eight-thirty on weekdays as long as I had finished my homework, but I always did my homework at school, while the teacher was still reciting what needed to be turned in the next day, I was already filling out worksheets, adding fractions, colouring in maps, diagramming sentences, writing texts, copying poems, whatever it was in order to spend more time with you (you who were also very studious and did your homework as you were supposed to, even if you had to stay up late in that home without curfews where you lived now). On weekends they let us stay up until nine (they let me until nine: you, as I said, were a free agent, you no longer had restrictions, just as you no longer had a mother). And in summer, even until ten. Nothing happened in that neighbourhood of Bilbao in the '80s (or a lot happened, but we didn't see it, nor did it affect us) we didn't stray further than three streets, we didn't cross more than one stoplight to go to the park alongside the Cadagua, which emptied into the ría of the Nervión a little bit further, in the industrial area. They didn't let us go to the industrial area, I suppose that in the '80s, and at night, everything had to be going on there.

We would head towards a shopping arcade, a pretentious name for what was nothing more than this sinister passage-way in which clumped together narrow little duty-free shops, key-copying places, shoe repairs, photocopyists, and even a confectionery, with three tables and a window looking onto the street. I don't know what we did there, nor how it was possible to spend so many hours there: we watched people wander, we spoke with some and with others, we played on the pinball machine (later—soon—Donkey Kong, Tetris, wha-tever they had). We got home smelling of photocopies. We never had a penny, or we spent it right away, so most of the time what we did was watch how others played: the tiny sweet shop full of hypnotized kids watching the games. Other times, if there were customers (middle-aged women who finished their shifts in the area shops, in the mattress factory, co-workers of your dead mothers, all very put together and with those hair dyes in hallucinogenic colours that are so noticeable outside of here) we went out into the street and watched through the window. When we grew bored, we went to sit in a doorway near your house to eat candies: fresones, balines, manzanitas, black and red gummy berries, liquorice disks. That night it rained cats and dogs, a strong rain that flooded the streets. The water flowed, dragging the trash towards the sewers, which backed up, and the cars also clogged the streets, like almost always, honking at one another under that sickly light. Dirty water dripped from the tops of the buildings. Sometimes we played at looking up (the higher floors disappeared among the low clouds) with our eyes open, hoping the drops would fall into our eyes.

You had a bit of something on your lips, something pink and crystalline that shone in the light of the street lamps. You kept talking about I don't know what, about what we always talked about, about what twelve- or thirteen-year-olds talk about, and I didn't stop watching that shiny pink thing on your lip. Although perhaps (and that is what I think now) what I watched were your lips and I don't know how I watched them, if I watched them with some intention. And you kept talking and talking without stopping, something rare in you, since you almost never talked, never spoke, and I no longer listened to you, but suddenly you had turned into your lips and only that existed, and I watched how they moved in slow motion in the darkness of that rainy night. And then I did what your mother would have done, what I would never have done before and probably should never have done because it made you withdraw, because it had painful consequences (or no, I'll never know, that's the bad thing about the past, that it is so difficult to go back and rectify it, to know if by doing something different everything would have happened the same): I wet my thumb with saliva and rubbed it against your lips to remove the clump of sugar for you.

You said that I was a jerk. That what I'd done was disgusting. That I was a pig. That the next time I should stick my finger up my butt. That I never do that to you again. That you were going to beat me to a pulp. That some kids from our class might have seen me do that, some of the kids from the galería comercial (we always said 'la galería comercial' as if that way we could explain better why we spent so much time there). What would happen if they'd seen us? How disgusting, by God. That I not touch you again. That I never touch you again. That if I was thinking that I was your mother, or that I would be your mother, then I better forget about it, that your mother was six feet under, she'd been eaten up by worms, that if they opened her coffin now she'd still have hair (short because she always wore it cut in a boy's style, because she never had time to even dry it, I'm sure, and that was the reason for her decision, which caused comments among her girlfriends—*honey, you're never going to get married again like that*—long hair is such a bother and, besides, in this city nothing ever dries), how, since she died, every night, every damned night, you only think of the coffin, of how she'd be tonight, whether her stomach had already exploded, if the bugs were eating her eyes, if her hands (those hands which had been so calming, which frightened off all your fears, which tickled) would now be just a few unsavoury bones (I'm sure you didn't use that word, that one I use now). That I leave you alone.

That I had no idea what it was like, being alone, that I couldn't even imagine it. Being orphaned. That I was a jerk. How disgusting. That I was a pig. That the next time I should stick my finger in my butt. And then you crouched down, you sat down on the step, you lowered your head as if you were dizzy, you grabbed your ears with your hands and began to rock back and forth and to cry slowly, almost without making a sound. I sat down next to you and hugged you. You put your head on my lap with your eyes closed. I didn't listen to you. I didn't listen to you and I touched you. Sometimes it's necessary not to listen to what people say because they want the opposite. I caressed your hair, which smelled of photocopies and coffee and glue from the soles of our shoes, as mine probably did as well, as the '80s now forever smelled in my memory. I dried your tears with my fingers, but you didn't stop crying. And it rained and we both got drenched. You started to hum that song your mother sang you: *hegoak ebaki banizkio nerea izango zen . . . hegoak ebaki banizkio nerea izango zen . . .*

Cars passed by and splashed us. In the distance, from high up, in some apartment lost among the clouds and the rain, a child could be heard crying. The yellow or red lights of the cars skated over your face and your tears shone by moments. I caressed your ears. Your neck, hair, hands. You grabbed tightly to my legs and kept singing and crying at the same time, thinking of your mother, of course, of your mother who worked as an accountant in a mattress factory from eight to five, who never showed up, some last-minute supplier wanting to be paid, some lost invoice, some frenetic boss who didn't understand that employees had private lives, or that there are always traffic jams when it rains, those narrow streets, all the cars on the road at the same time just then, cars double and triple parked. Of your mother who now would never drink a coffee with her middle-aged girlfriends in the confectionery of the galería comercial when they got off work, of your mother who had never done that because she never had time, because she never even had time to dry her hair. You asked me if I was a jerk, but now you were smiling. How disgusting, but smiling. That I was a pig, and you laughed. That the next time I should stick my finger up my butt, and now I smiled, from how hurt I was. That I should never do that again, and we both laughed. That you'd beat me to a pulp, cackling. That if one of our class-mates had seen me do it, you wept and laughed. What would happen if they saw us, crying and laughing, both of us at the same time. How disgusting, by God, rolling on the ground, cracking up. That I never touch you again, and I was already touching you, tickling you. That I never touch you ever again, and I sucked my thumb and rubbed it over your lips.

The worst thing of all is the light of November because night falls very quickly, and then it's an orange light, the light of the street lamps. But it's not a light that evokes oranges or mandarins: it's a light of hospitals, of industrial estates, of ring roads, a light of burials, of a dead mother, of her decomposing body, a light also of the death of my own father, years later, much later, orphaned of my father much later than you, I understood something then (not everything: it's impossible to understand the orphanhood of a child, impossible to under-stand it for those of us who've never been orphaned children but adult orphans), I understood something then about what you felt many years before, in a dark doorway under a heavy rain that flooded the streets while the water flowed, dragging the trash towards the sewers, which backed up, and the cars also clogged the streets, like almost always, honking at one another under that sickly light. But the worst, perhaps the worst thing of all, was the unsavoury light of the galería comercial, as unsavoury as the bones of the hands of your dead mother. Despite being certain that unsavoury was not a word you'd use then, and I'm almost sure that you don't use it now because unsavoury is a word that only those who write use, because it's pretty and because it makes one think and one comes to forget about the bones and the light of the galería comercial and you repeat unsavoury a few times until it loses all meaning, as always happens when something repeats, as always happens when you spend a long time looking at the face of someone close to you, until you don't recognize it, and then one comes to think that we move through the world only glancingly, that we read diagonally, that we look out of the corners of our eyes because, if every time we concentrate on something it loses the meaning it had for us until that moment, then it means we were wrong, that we are always wrong because we're full throttle and never have time for anything, and we create a simple world, a simplified one, a world that's not the one that exists, but a version in our own fashion of the world, for our convenience, and this happens with everything, with those names they give us, with those names we give others, with those adjectives we use to label ourselves, with those adjectives we use to label others. Perhaps writing is nothing more than a way of approaching the complexity of the world, perhaps spending two afternoons to recount three minutes of real life is nothing more than that attempt to understand that world in which we don't have time to live, perhaps it's nothing more than a vain intent.

I wrote: 'I walk barefoot and I twist upon ice clouds. The afternoon passes through the window and leaves golden threads among the net curtains. The light of autumn disperses the sighs of boredom. On the table, a cup of coffee wakes the ghosts of the siesta. What are you doing there? I look. I look at life in the dirty window, look at how time dilutes among the grey clouds heavy with water, I look at the other windows on the street spilling light from dining rooms and bedrooms, from lavatories, from night-time baths for infants, relaxing showers of husbands who return late, an old woman's for-gotten kitchen, light of tortilla, light of lightly boiled eggs, of freshly ironed white clothes, light that unveils the last drunks on the street, I look at the cold night that approaches with its claws and uncut nails, full of grime, I hear their harsh scrape against the walls, feel their cold beating, its hidden skull behind the habits, its satisfied delight when it sees me tremble, I hear it laugh when it tears off the head of a drunk, when it drinks their intoxicating blood, blood of cheap rum, of bad wine and lukewarm beer. I look at the steps that open before me, which descend towards an abyss of my own, towards myself, and I go down towards my insides stumbling over bodies of dead animals, rotting lichens, and poisonous plants. Today the sky glimmers a yellowish-grey, covered by an infi-nite enormous dirty cloud, studded by sudden glimmers of dying light that escape at intervals from between the chinks of half-open windows in glass-and-aluminium skyscrapers, crossing dark branches of dry poplars to which the last withered yellow leaves cling, trembling weakly in the frozen wind like dangling banners in some moribund fair. Today there isn't even a colourless rain that slides subtly through the windows, nor puddles of shadowy gloom between the dark walks, not even damp flagstones that reflect no steel light, nor people getting lost down alleyways of intoxicated fog. Today I lug the grief of not being able to say the unsayable, fighting with the anguish of being and not wanting to be, of sinking into oblivion forever or of turning back, before even being, before myself, where there is not even oblivion. Life breaks loose from the poplars in tatters, and the branches, outlined in green-black shadows, shrink inward in their extinction of dying rapture, paralysed, surprised by the cold of November, overwhelmed in its frozen casket of gargoyles and waits. Life dies on the paths, death whirls in dirty suburban corners and sometimes takes flight, rising in a final numb trembling, to weaken and descend in tornados of ice. Green life dies and it is so beautiful, it dies at last, burnt, the final paroxysm of summer, and an ominous luminosity of despair and doubt spreads its faltering halitosis through the empty streets. Don't collect the fallen leaves! Let us contemplate the yellow beauty of death.'

Monday, 18 August 2014.
Beach. Alubias. Getxo

Once again it dawns a sunny day and we decide to return to the beach. For Tuesday they're predicting rain, so we might not see the sun again for the rest of the week. The walk from the Larrabasterra metro to the beach, perhaps two kilometres, is very pleasant. They're building a lot of houses in the area since a few years ago, but they're not ugly. One can still inhale the scent of countryside, the silence and the calm. Before, one went over a river that has now disappeared. Any day it will appear once more, during some torrential rain, and it will carry off some semi-detached. We never learn. It's not too hot, in fact a slight breeze has sprung up and we fear we won't be able to lie out for very long on the beach.

'And you? Are you going to be you?'

'Of course not, I can't be myself except in some partial way, a portion, as I told you. It is hard enough to be me in daily life to have to also be me in a novel. So probably I'll often say things that are not true, or that I don't know if they're true, or which I don't think, or which I want to believe I don't think simply because that's convenient for me, to carry on the thread of the dialogue, to make you think (if, that is, you are not my other me) because you make me think, because in that way perhaps we understand something or come to some conclusion or we make someone reflect or consider or reconsider something, and to make perhaps some conclusion also much better than our own. That helps us to make our conclusions mine.'

'In other words, we can't trust that you are you, either.'

'Of course not. But that's true in general, in life, in any conversation, in any piece of writing whether it's autobiographical or not, in any document no matter how many signatures it has.'

We walk in silence for a good while, each of us lost in our thoughts. When we're going down towards the beach, you ask me how, if after much reflection, you would have understood something. Or perhaps you're just being kind, as you've almost always been, showing an interest in my crap.

'But what you talk about, is it romantic love, love like what a normal couple feels?'

'What for you is normal?'

'Don't confuse me.'

'Let's take a look . . . What do I know? Is the love that a mother has for her child, a brother for his sister, a son for his father—is that a different love from romantic love?'

'Well, in principle it's different because there's no sex, there's no sexual desire involved.'

'I'll accept that. In principle that's how it is. Well, the same thing happens with Edorta and Koldo.'

'They love one another like brothers.'

'But not like brothers—that's the problem.'

'Why is that a problem?'

'Because our culture accepts the love between siblings, between parents and children as something natural. It's natural for them to love one another extremely, that they be able to give their life for one another. However, loves between friends—especially if they are men—are condemned to failure and are not looked upon favourably. They might be accepted in childhood, and even into adolescence, but not after. After that, it's a mistake, something sick, something that affects their adult life, something that can't be shared with other kinds of loves.'

'Especially if they're both men?'

'I have the feeling (but it could be the machoism that permeates me since the day I came into this world and from which I try to flee) that the love between two female friends is not viewed as badly, that it has historically been tolerated always so long as there was no suspicion of lesbianism (something that never existed, given that sex between two women was inconceivable).'

'Go on, keep talking.'

'If I, as I've already said before, don't give the slightest importance to sex, why does sex need to be decisive in the love between two men to such a degree that if they have it, it converts them immediately into homosexuals, and if they don't have it, they aren't homosexuals, although there always exists from the outside the suspicion that yes, that they are, that they don't dare, that they haven't come out of the closet?'

'Koldo and Edorta love each other.'

'Tremendously, I hope to make that clear.'

'And they don't desire one another sexually.'

'They don't want to fuck. Let's call things by their names. They don't have that need. Just as two brothers don't have it (there's much to talk about in this regard, but I think it's not common, although that isn't to deny that it happens nor needless to say I am criticizing it), nor a father with his children . . .'

I shut up because one need only read the daily newspaper to see that this is not so.

'Now you've put your foot in your mouth.'

You take advantage of the moment to tease me. But it's the only way of understanding: to try and make the other understand what you want to understand and which escapes you.

We sit on the sand to rest. After a while, we start to wander down the beach, but the day doesn't seem like it's going to get much better, we've put on our shirts but even so it's a bit chilly. Since it's almost lunchtime, we decide to look for somewhere (not even the chiringuito has opened). We catch the train and get off at a stop near the old port of Algorta: at this time of day everything is very lively, the terrazas are full and people are having a pre-meal drink. Despite it being a Monday; I guess many people are on vacation. We find a restaurant which offers 'beans from Tolosa with all its sacraments' and we can't resist the temptation to try them. The dining room is on the upper floor, an airy space with peaked roofs and exposed dark wooden beams, decorated with seascapes (not especially delicate ones) and model ships and other objects with a vaguely nautical appearance: golden compasses, white ropes, polished wooden rudders. The beans are served in a clay pot with green guindillas (piparras, I think they're called). I thought that the sacraments were the guindillas but no, the seven sacraments are inside the dish: onion, pepper, morcilla, chorizo, tocino, jamón, and bacon.

After, we wander down through the old port towards the beach. It's cloudy, but the wind has calmed down. I've got an itch to go into the water thinking that perhaps it will be the last swim of the week, of these holidays. You sit down on some concrete blocks near the showers to read, while I take off my clothes and slide into the almost-waveless water in that closed bay. There is no one there, not even on the maritime boardwalk. The water isn't cold, it's probably even warmer than the air. That wouldn't be strange. Now the sun comes out again and a few groups of young people come down to the beach: Germans, Dutch. Blond-haired and reddish-skinned. Restless, jumpy, but they don't make noise. The beach is empty and any noise, any shout, seems an outburst. They know how to keep silent, these youth, they respect our tranquillity (yours, reading, now that you've come down to the shore and you've also taken off your clothes and you're reading on a towel). Like entering a church, or a living room in which the owners of the house are asleep in front of the TV.

In Gunnersbury Park
(The Hit Parade, Sarah Records 058, 1991)

you can hear the trees sigh as they watch the lovers pass them
If my hands could reach you know I would not let go

The worst thing of all is the light of the locker room, especially in autumn, when daylight saving ends, and now as early as four, and if it's cloudy outside, the lights need to be turned on because through the frosted glass only a weak greyish light slips in from the street. And there is always some fluorescent bulb that flickers and emits intermittent clicks. That is the worst thing of all. I am there only because all the boys have already left, but I always wait for you because you're one of the few who showers at the gym (who knows if it's to save on hot water, to forget the dampness of your home, to not have to wait your turn in that bathroom you share among four almost-adults). We're fifteen now and we're hombrecitos, almost real men, that's what your aunt says. It smells of chlorine, of bleach, of socks, of deodorant, of sweat. Through the windows seeps the ruckus of the others who, until a moment ago, wandered through here slapping one another, giving wedgies to José María, the petite mariquita, and it seems like their voices still echo among the green tiles. I'm seated on a wooden bench, already putting on my clothes to go out onto the street. A black sweatshirt jacket has been forgotten on a hanger. It's the mandatory school uniform: an orange T-shirt and a black sweatshirt. It's not totally ugly, but people don't usually like the orange. When we compete against other schools, they call us the butaneros, because our shirts are the orange of butane tanks. I hear the water of the incessant shower, it seems you never want it to stop, perhaps so as not to see the others, or so they don't see you naked. Other times I think you do it so that we remain alone in this territory that's so ours, so only for boys. Now our life is full of people, of girls, girls everywhere, now we don't even sit together. Girls in class, at recess, in the gang of friends. Here, in the locker room, it seems like we regain a bit of what we lost, of our afternoons. I hear the shower has stopped. Steam has fogged the mirrors and I approach one of them to wipe it with a towel so that I'm able to comb my hair. I've got a lot of hair and there's always a rebel cowlick that my mother hates, that is the bane of my amatxu in the mornings. I see you reflected in the mirror. You appear naked, barefoot, and you sit beside me on the bench where we always sit. There, on the rack, your clothes are hanging. We don't have lockers, but there's never any need. We show up, leave everything hanging, all jumbled, on the benches or the floor, some more organized than others, everywhere full of backpacks, sneakers, jackets, shirts. You grab the towel you've got tucked in your backpack (you are very careful, perhaps the aunt who acts as your mother needs some control over her life and that of the three adoptive or adopted sons, a kind of control which my family, without going any further, is unaware of). It's a tiny bath towel, pink in colour. Maybe that's why you don't want to come out while the others are here like a herd. You dry yourself carefully and apply this greenish-white powder (to protect against fungus, I think you told me once) on your armpits, your balls, and your feet. You pull out some underwear, white underwear with little drawings, like the ones common back then, the kind one doesn't see any more, and you get dressed slowly. You dry your chest with the towel and you look at me. You smile. Like what you see or what? you say laughing. And then, with the wet towel, you snap me on the butt, leaving it red all after-noon. And I'm already dressed. Then I turn around and run towards you, already on your way back to the wooden bench as if you don't expect anything, as if you didn't know that the same things would happen as happens every gym afternoon when the worst thing of all is the weak greyish light that slips in from the street and the flickering bulb, as if you weren't wanting it, and I throw myself at you and grab you by the neck, and with my knees I make you lose your balance and fall on your back to the ground, so cold, so wet. And I sit on top of you, grabbing you by the neck, aware of your dick through your underwear (however, I never felt the slightest curiosity about your dick, not greater than for your neck, your ears, your nose). You twist under me and kick. But I am already dressed and wearing shoes and I'm stronger. Give up, I tell you, give up, cowboy, give up, scoundrel. But you hold on, you kick more, you even spit at me, bite my arm. Give up, coward, give up or face the Chinese torture of Fu Manchu. You shout: No. No. And you die of laughter and fear. Then I grab your legs a bit above the knee and squeeze tightly with my fingers, and a delicious and brutal shock flows through your body.

No, please, I can't bear it, I give up, I give up. And you close your eyes and start to breathe deeply. Good dog, dog dog, I tell you as I gently caress your wet hair. Now what am I going to do with this dripping underwear? you say. The same as every day, guarro. You're well aware that your aunt (even your poor mother, a widow and dead) would be horrified if you put your pants on over your wet underwear. Then you'll catch pneumonia, die, and what do I do then? What shall I do if you die? she tells you, the other would tell you. So you undress once more and put on your sweats with nothing on underneath. You can see everything, I tell you, if you get a woodie you'll see how funny it'll be. If Itziar should see you, you'll see how funny it is. You'll be like a tent pole. I don't get hard with Itziar, that's you, do you think we're idiots? And perhaps he's right because I do like Itziar, I like how she laughs, because when she laughs it seems it's always June, the final days of school, when they leave us the afternoon free or organize some dance. We won't see her anyway, I tell you. The girls have already left a while ago. It's only since you're such a blockhead that we're the last ones here. If we don't hurry they'll close the door and we'll be stuck here all night. You'd really like that, you little maricón, you tell me. It's strange because, since then, since those gym afternoons on which the worst thing of all was the light of the blinking fluorescent bulb, you've almost never joked with me about the matter, as if you feared that there was some truth to it, as if you feared that you or I, or both of us, were maricones, like Josemari. I have always been sure, sure that I wasn't. That in one of those struggles with you, when you were half-naked, I would have noticed some kind of sexual excitement, something exclusively related to physical aspects, let's say, with the proximity of flesh, with the force applied to specific points, with the brush of intimate parts, exactly the same that I noticed, sometimes, your hard cock brushing my ass when I sat on top of you. But I never masturbated thinking of you, nor did I have dreams or erotic fantasies with you. I masturbated to Victoria Vera, to Victoria Abril. I guess it was the same with you. But I can only speak of myself, I don't know what things went through your head then, that's how adolescence is, it's as if the world opens like a full mini bar in an all-included hotel, I don't even know what happened then nor what's happening to you now, now that we hardly ever see each other.

We go out into the street and, sure enough, there's no one left. You still have wet hair and it's night and the moon reflects off your head, shining. I want to touch your hair, but you don't deal with that well, you no longer deal with it well that I do things like that, only that we fight, only fighting. No, of course not there, in the street, where everyone could see us. Although I know that you want it, I know you're yearning for it. Now no one caresses your hair nor gives you their hand, nor puts their hand on your head when you have a fever. A motorcycle passes making noise. Some seagulls squawk around the piles of trash beside the ría. A car trapped by a double-parked motorist honks. An ambulance heads towards Cruces, towards where the 'critical burn unit' is. I always shiver when I hear that: critical burn unit. Perhaps in that ambulance is someone with critical burns. Some bushes let fall the final leaves they have left. A man with a Guardia Civil tracksuit walks a black dog. One hears the noise of the factories and a column of black smoke ('it's not smoke, it's vapour!' you always say) mingles among the low clouds that seem close and orange by the light of the street lamps. The rush of the Cadagua presages the next swelling. One of these summers it will overflow—and the Nervión ría too—and flood all of Bilbao.

I write: 'I woke one night and contemplated my life stretching before me like a grey hallway without side doors, with death just at the end, without any chance of escape, dirty grey adult life, in a suit and tie smelling of the office, my saliva now always tasting of photocopies, keyboards, and printer ink, afternoons of murky clouds and sickly yellowish light that filters through semi-opaque windows closed shut like tombs, always breathing the same air now, our own recycled breath that passes through dusty tubes full of rats and dead pigeons, our sweat of projected death, our slow decay, our weariness, already defeated. Behind the unforeseeable days, the promises of love, the future like a box full of rusty handles, of secret drawers, with saliva that tastes of sweet moss and yellow flowers, whenever everything could still be. Only the hallway remains.'

Tuesday, 19 August 2014.
Durango. Elorrio. Tortilla de bacalao

'And all that business with the albums, with the music?'

'You mean Sarah Records? You can't even imagine how important those songs were in my life. Sometimes I think I am how I am thanks to them.'

'But, does anyone know those albums?'

'Well, that's part of the emotion. It's like a treasure. Certainly, it's usually gratifying to share things with others, but the emotion diminishes when the others are many in number, it depreciates. And trust me, I did everything possible to share them, but there was no way to do so. I like to think that I do so now, and I think it's not too late.'

'But why now, in this story?'

'It's more a feeling than anything else. When I listened to those songs, when I looked at those covers, when I read those lyrics, when I tried to translate them, I felt things that took me out of my world, a kind of nostalgia for something that hasn't been lost because I never had it. Can one have nostalgia for things that have not happened? (That was asked in some film.) I think you can. Those songs spoke to me of English coastal towns, of rain and fog, of empty, desolate beaches, of those streets with squat houses and a little garden, of floors with moquette and stairways. Of little parks in working-class neighbourhoods where people go for a walk as soon as there's the slightest bit of sunlight. An empty street and some parked cars with white numbers on black licence plates.'

'And that's why it's set in Bilbao.'

'At least the light is similar.'

'The worst of Bilbao is the light.'

'The worst thing of all is the light.'

'I see you already have the title.'

'I always have the title early on.'

'They'll say that worse than the light is the gas bill or the phone bill.'

'I'm counting on it. But it's not the truth. The light is worse.'

'There's a novel by Ray Loriga called *Lo peor de todo*.'

'I know. They'd be next to each other if books were lined up alphabetically by title. But books are almost never ordered that way.'

We'd been told it would be a lousy day, so we've decided to go on an excursion to Durango. It's been years since we last visited. There's a lot of commotion at the Bilbao bus station, like almost every summer. But what's more, at the hospital of Basurto, next door, there are tons of TV cameras because of a supposed case of Ebola. We catch the bus to Durango and arrive quickly, there's almost no traffic and the sun is shining. The mountains near Durango have always moved me. We head to the tourism office to get a map, they show us a route we can follow to visit the most important sites. There's a pretty view from the river, a plaza with terrazas where people have breakfast in the sun beside a famous gate, under the tower of the church, surrounded by manors with reddish peaked roofs. The river gentles into a small pond which reflects the gate and the tower. In other areas, the river flows dark between households that sink their musty foundations into the current. Some of them, painted in bright colours, evoke Gerona (perhaps also Venice or Florence). But I've always been of the opinion that cities shouldn't be compared, so I prefer to keep quiet. Besides, I know that you adore Durango and its surroundings. I'd like to take a walk towards the mountain. They've shown us a few routes, but they keep insisting that a storm is brewing and we're not prepared to be caught out by strong rains on the mountain.

In the door of the Banco de Santander is a really handsome man. He's staring at his phone, standing beside two bikes, wearing a red-and-white T-shirt and those black pants typical of cyclists.

'Look at him.'

'Is he one of them?'

'He could be Koldo at twenty-five.'

'And the other bike?'

'Edorta is in the bank, inside. Taking care of something. They've gone out for a spin from Bilbao and have arrived in Durango. Surely they need to get home for lunch.'

'And aren't there banks in Bilbao? Why do they need to come to Durango?'

'Let's see. Yes, there are banks, but they open in the afternoon and these two want to wake early to go on this trip together. Haven't I already told you that time is important for them, that scant time they steal from their families?'

'Are they already married with kids?'

'No, I don't think so. But Edorta is probably already busy with the headaches of the wedding. Maybe he needs to send a wire transfer to reserve the reception. And Koldo is sending messages to his girlfriend. Perhaps he's also already thinking of the wedding. Of the few outings together and alone that they have left.'

I've posted a photo of the cyclist on Facebook and Instagram, you can't see his face and he's far away, but right away my phone has begun to vibrate with appreciative comments. I think I've chosen Koldo well.

We turn back towards the bus station and the sky starts to cloud over. We think about eating in Durango, depending on the next bus to Elorrio which no one seems clear about. Someone tells us it will arrive soon, so we decide to wait for the bus and eat in Elorrio.

When we get there, everything seems rather quiet and isolated. We go into the main church, the Purísima Concepción, one of those Hallenkirche temples you like so much. The ribbing of the gothic vault sketch clear, elegant lines in the air and the purity of the floor leads us to stay inside a long time despite being hungry. When we come outside, a young man points us in the direction of a bar on the outskirts that we reach in a few minutes. There we eat a tortilla de bacalao sandwich I can still remember (and it still makes my mother water) seated on the terraza, looking at the mountain, facing a group of new houses that don't fit in very well with the setting. However, they must have a great view from their bay windows, of the church, the old part of Elorrio and its palaces, and the mountains. It's unquestionably threatening to rain but we decide to follow a path that leads to the Argiñeta necropolis, a group of anthropomorphic sarcophagi and funeral steles from the High

Middle Ages with inscriptions, which I remembered having visited on one of our first summers. (I've kept a photo of you from then, standing in front of the sarcophagi, perhaps from 1996 or around that time.) The place is magical and the arboretum gives off a green luminosity that accentuates the sensation of unreality. Even more so now that no one is around and the black clouds have darkened the entire sky. Some of the inscriptions read rather well.

'*In Dei Nomine Momus in corpore bibentem . . .*'

'It says all that?'

'And more: *mi fecit. Ic dormit.*'

'He made me. He sleeps here. And without even knowing Latin.'

We go back towards the town, passing before some little houses with tiny plots that are full of flowers among the vegetables, like comestible gardens. We cross some summer tourists, the kind that always make me feel jealous, those who return year after year to the same house in the North and have time to even grow bored (something that would be marvellous to me because they remind me the eternal summers of childhood when you go back each year to the same place, that place where you've already seen everything, where you've discovered everything, and the only thing you do is see it all once more, to re-encounter perhaps who you were just one year before, as if you could go back in time through repetitions). Back in Elorrio, we take a walk along the main street, full of palaces, and along the parallel streets to see the patios of the stately manors from the back gates.

After drinking a coffee at the bar in the plaza, we go back towards the bus. I fall asleep—I almost always sleep on buses, trains, planes. Never in cars (I'm afraid of cars). I'm woken by a thunderclap, and on opening my eyes, I see the highway drenched by the foretold downpour. It looks like the asphalt boils in little bubbles of water. Inside the bus, the windows have fogged up and it's stuffy. In the distance, on the Vizcaya coast, a yellowish glimmer announces that the storm won't last for too long. At least for today.

It's Only Obvious

(The Orchids, Sarah Records 401, 1989)

who needs tomorrow, when all I need, all I needed was you

The worst thing of all is the light of the street on which you live because it's always the same. The cars parked haphazardly, double parked, in front of the bakery. The light of the bakery itself on winter afternoons when the little kids get out of school (perhaps, because of the hour, it's instead when they get out of English lessons, ballet lessons, swim class, piano lessons, rhythmic gymnastics, flute lessons, judo lessons, Basque dancing classes) and they clump together in front of the loaves of bread, the pastries, the glazed doughnuts, the chocolate palmeras. The upper floors disappear upwards into the night and there are some lights, still few, from the high terrazas. The number of times I've waited for you there, leaning or perhaps sitting on some car, the number of times I've set off one of their alarms!

Today I've been waiting for you in the doorway. You can't imagine how happy I feel at these moments when I know I am going to see you right away. The happiness is comparable to the sadness your absences causes me on those weekends when your aunt takes the car, stuffs all three of you by force into it because you don't want to go, and you set off for Burgos to see your grandfather, your father's father, so you don't lose contact, always so difficult to keep going when the person connecting you has died. It's Friday and we've arranged to meet to go for a spin, to go to the rec centre, a dark hall in which they play pool and foosball in the back, while in the front area there's a line of pinball machines and a few video games: Pacman, Alien, 1942, Donkey Kong, Arkanoid. I don't usually pay them much attention, but I like to see you handling the controls, see how you get so angry when some Martian kills you. When we don't have any money (which is usually half an hour after we get there) we go into the back where the older kids play billiards and smoke cigarettes and joints. It stinks of sweat and piss because there's a bathroom nearby, always so filthy I prefer to go in the street, between two cars, wherever. When I play pinball, which is the one I like best, you place your hand on my shoulder, you stand very close to me and even press hard, pushing against me, as if I were just a puppet and you were pulling my strings. You smell of watermelon gum. In the back, next to the pool table, there's a little stand that sells cigarettes, Bazooka gum, Palotes, pica-pica, Kojak Chupa Chups, bailes, and fresones, and these smell good—of strawberry, of liquorice, of tobacco. The woman who runs it is a thousand years old and is always half-asleep, but she never misses a thing. If she can get away with it, she short-changes you. She also makes change for the machines. Before, there were machines to break bills into coins, but someone discovered a way to make it give you change without putting anything in. It was ruinous for business so they had to shut it down, to the joy of the woman at her stand, who enjoys handling the money. There are four enormous pool tables and now they've put in one of American billiards, smaller, and more appreciated by those like me who can't manage even a carom in classic pool. On the American table, it's rare that I don't manage to sink *some* ball, whether or not it's one of those I'm supposed to. You're strange today. Thoughtful, and you only smile from half your mouth. I don't know what's worrying you. Perhaps there are money problems at home (but there almost always are). They might have become more pressing. At the door are Itziar and Claudia. You like Claudia. They, needless to say, don't come inside rec centres. They're waiting for us to go and sit in the park, next to the river, which is now dark and isolated, even though it's just seven in the evening. We usually go there with them to neck for a while, the four of us seated on the same bench, to touch their tits. You kiss with lots of saliva, and your deep kisses go on really long. Claudia wipes her lips with her hands between each kiss because your saliva drips down her chin. You get a hard-on right away, you jab me with your elbow, with your eyes you lead my gaze towards your pants, the pants of your school uniform (you haven't even changed, at your home the clothes don't dry), a grey pair of pants that now seems like a ship under full sail.

Claudia says that you're a pervert, but she leans in for another deep kiss. We've never made out, you and I, despite the fact that at some moments I'd have liked to kiss you, on the cheek, near your lips. We have jerked off together, of course, like everyone does. First we started by touching one another's dicks, out of pure curiosity, but without being excited, like playing doctor, pure anatomy, then we discovered the whole business of masturbation (I don't even remember who was the one who started, perhaps we both discovered it at the same time, those things are like gunpowder), each with his own at first and then lending each other a hand, close your eyes and think that I'm Itziar, close your eyes and think that I'm Victoria Vera, close your eyes and think that I'm Victoria Abril, close your eyes and think that I'm Bárbara Rey. At first we came and no semen came out, just some little white dots, like dust, or flour, we were that small. The first time we ejaculated as adults was simultaneously, for some mysterious reason I never understood. Two enormous orgasms that left both of us surprised and frightened at the same time.

Itziar and Claudia leave, they have to go early, and we approach the ría. It's dark and you remain dark. When you're like this I'd rather leave you, for you to go off on your own, it's usually counterproductive. The worst thing of all is that these moments last for increasingly longer and are not logical. I always thought that being a kid was the worst, that when we were adults—at least when we were young—we'd have everything in our hands, without any prohibitions any more, with money in our pockets. We'd get drunk if we felt like it, grab the car and go to the beach to sleep with both of them, to have sex in the sand, all four of us together, with the moon on the black horizon and the sound of the waves battering our feet. To grab the car and go to Burgos, to Santander, to Donosti, to some discotheque where nobody knew us. To get drunk on cheap cubatas, the kind that kill you, to dance beneath the mirrored balls, the four of us clutching on to one another, braying the refrains in English. We'd buy albums. We'd go to London. I, especially, wanted to go to London, for us to go to London.

I write: 'Love lives on the skin of your large, warm hands dampening your caresses of virgin light. Love lives in your steel eyes, in the coppery taste of your iris, and it reverberates like the water of August in the ocean. Save me, Love! Rock me in your hands! Let me lose myself, that I am flooded by your foam, that I drown in your smoke, that I burn up in your violet fire! Caress me at the dawn.

'What do you know of love when you lower your gaze towards the pavement? What would you know of love when you smile in such a stupid way, like someone who laughs at a kid, like someone who laughs at a dog? What do you know of love no matter that you've got kids (forgotten), or that your kids have kids? What would you know of love when you disdain the only thing that's sacred? What would you know of love? Have you ever seen it? Felt some time its bitter embrace, its tenuous stabbing, its passioned death? What would you know of love? Oh, you forgot. Death is always better than oblivion.

'Get out of here, Love, and wait for me in the shadows, I still want to enjoy the sun even if it burns me. Breathe deep and rest. I want to prolong this agony for a century, this dissolution of sweet death, of ecstatic sacrifice, of painful pleasure, let me enjoy this chimera. Get out of here, Love, and wait for me in the shadows, resuscitate, catch your breath, we've still got long journeys to make. I prefer to endure even if it's for a century, I'll catch my breath later, I'll perfume myself later with crystalline amber, let me agonize and die even if it's for a kiss. Get out of here, Love, and wait for me in the shadows.'

Wednesday, 20 August 2014.
Museums. Rain. Plentzia

'And what about ETA? A novel that takes place in Euskadi during the past forty years and you're not going to talk about the infamous Basque separatist group?'

'Well, ETA isn't just something of the Basque Country. And not all the novels of the world talk of ETA. Not even all the novels of Spain. Sorry, of the Spanish state.'

'But people won't understand. They'll think your silence is eloquent.'

'I don't care. The same thing always happens with ETA. But it happens with lots of things lately: people defend ideas with the fanaticism of a fundamentalist, of someone enlightened, with blind faith. Then they're fiercely critical of believers, of Muslims, of Catholics, but it happens with dogs, for example. The dialogue is simplified, it reaches a level of zero tolerance. All of us who don't believe the way you do are terrorists. That's why I'm increasingly less willing to dialogue.'

'In any event, you'll be speaking of ETA if you transcribe this conversation.'

'If I transcribe it. It's a way of at least saying that I've thought this, that I've thought about it. And that it doesn't interest me, that I didn't want to distract attention. ETA is like the muleta waved before the bull so that he charges.'

'And don't you think that with these dialogues, with the novel's duplicate structure, with the whole issue of Sarah Records, with Blas de Otero, with the photos, with the diaries whether or not they're written a posteriori, that you're doing precisely the opposite, getting sidetracked from the subject?'

'Blas de Otero? You already know that I'm going to talk about Blas de Otero?'

'And about Proust. Undoubtedly.'

I fall silent for a while thinking about whether you're right, thinking that you're right. Like almost always. Like always.

You continue, 'I'd put something about ETA in the life of Edorta and Koldo. Elided, like the rest of important events.'

'I don't know. I don't see it clearly. I'm in favour of the rights of prisoners, of all prisoners, in all countries, no matter what they've done. The final goal is social reinsertion. I've been called a terrorist for saying that, for saying that I'm in favour of rapprochement. Can you imagine? I prefer not to speak.'

'The zero degree of dialogue.'

'And my parents and my little sister could've died in the attack on Correo street in Madrid. Friday, 13 September 1974. I still remember spots of blood on my sister's flowered dress.'

'So you see.'

'Even so, maybe I will put something in, a single phrase. Perhaps one of Koldo's brothers wound up imprisoned in a jail in La Mancha. Or in Huelva. And Koldo went to visit him from time to time.'

'I'd put it in. It will seem like you don't want to talk about it and that will be strange: as if you were denying reality.'

'What will be strange is that my refusal to speak about ETA winds up occupying an entire dialogue.'

'Excusatio non petita.'

'Fuck them. Literally.'

'You know that "fuck them" will be misinterpreted, right? By some, by others, by the media.'

'I don't care. Fuck them all. It's my novel. I am in my "fuck them" phase. Before, I wasn't interested in the zero degree of the dialogue, nor in simplification of anything. But now . . .'

'But this novel is convoluted, no? Especially because of the subject. I don't even know what you're going to say when they ask you what it's about.'

'I won't say anything. It's all written here. The world is very complex and not wanting to see the complexity of the world is to lie.'

'And, then, in saying "fuck them". . . . aren't you entering their territory, that of the zero degree of dialogue?'

'It's a tantrum. In principle I don't want to explain the complexity of the world to anyone, especially if they don't want to understand it. If they don't want to, that's on them. Perhaps my revenge is the novel. Or my apology for not dialoguing.'

Today it's raining plenty and is cold. At least in the morning. They say that the sun will surely come out for a while in the afternoon. We've taken a bus that leads us near the Guggenheim. We almost always visit the temporary exhibits that are on in summer. There's usually not much of a queue to begin with. But, since it's raining today, we need to wait for around twenty minutes to get in. After, we head to the Museum of Fine Arts, which I love. Basque painting, primarily, which can't be seen anywhere else. I'm fascinated by the Zubiaurre brothers (those deaf faggots, someone once said) and, above all, Aurelio Arteta. I've been looking at those paintings for years, sometimes they change where they're hung, or one of those I'm looking for disappears. I always have the feeling that they remove some, or that, in my memory, there were more paintings, or that they were larger, or prettier. Or more homoerotic. 'Homoerotic Melancholy in Basque Costumbrist Painting'— my PhD dissertation could be called this when I wrote it, if I wrote it. Although perhaps I was the only one who felt that homoerotic melancholy, the fascination for the bodies of the arrantzales, of the baserritarras–the fisherman, the farmers. The same fascination that I felt (that I feel) for your body, of course. I also like very much the sophisticated painting of José María de Ucelay, so distant from the others as if they'd lived in different universes, perhaps they did (as perhaps we do now, in general, everyone and everywhere): ballet, afternoon snacks of tea and pastries, the chairs, the tables, the forged iron benches, the glassware that shone with the setting sun . . .

'It fits like a hand in a glove, the question of Basque painting. For your novel, I mean.'

'You're correct. I can't stop thinking of how many of these paintings tell things that aren't spoken with words.'

'Taste, gratification, complacency . . .'

'. . . the pleasure in contemplating the male body,' I interrupt you.

'You're obsessed.'

'I don't think so. It's they who were (who are) obsessed with the beauty of the male body and are unable to say so for fear of being tarred by what they are not, or what they don't want to be, or what they don't know if they are, or about which they have doubts. Of being labelled with a name when they think or know that what's happening to them is something else.'

'You think that one can love, can enjoy the beauty of the male body, without being a homosexual?'

'Of course. As I can enjoy the beauty of the female body. The problem lies in refusing oneself that pleasure. They're not able to admit it. The stereotypes tied to their gender forbid it. They usually disguise it with sport: when sports are involved, it's permissible to enjoy male bodies without any sort of guilt.'

'I don't know, I don't see it so simply. Do you think that all men enjoy the beauty of male bodies?'

'Now look. I don't know if all, but many of them indeed do. What I'm saying is that I'd like if they could do so freely. That there are bodies (of various kinds, not just the ones that fashion dictates at every moment) that are aesthetically enjoyable. But there are many men who don't enjoy them not because they don't want to nor because they aren't eager to, but out of fear, from fear.'

'So then, Arteta, Ucelay, and the Zubiaurre brothers weren't homosexuals?'

'I don't know if they were or not, nor do I care. I admire them because they don't have (they didn't have) any fear in enjoying and making others enjoy the beauty of Basque men— even if expressing it through painting and not in words. Look at the sculptures of Quintín de la Torre. The one of the cabin boy is a delight. Or the one of the loader.'

'And you think that this happens more in the Basque Country, in Basque painting, than elsewhere?'

'I haven't written my dissertation. I'd like to. But it's obvious that there is something, I don't know if it is cultural and has to do with the matriarchy, with the way of being Basque men have, if it's true that there is a way of being for Basque men, which I think there is . . .'

'And I am the living proof.'

'No need to tell me after living with you for twenty years. Let me go on: or if it has more with seeing the objective beauty of the Basque man, with the contact with nature, with the sea, with professions that demand physical effort, with the exhibition of their nudity. Something that in La Mancha, for example, we never see, or we rarely see: both the extreme heat as well as the extreme cold limit nudity. Come on, let's look for Julián de Tellaeche, we never find it.'

'They must have it hidden. Look, there are the José Arrues. They're marvels.'

'Yes. But butts like the ones Arteta painted have not existed in all of art history.'

'Perhaps you should call things clearly by their names and write a dissertation about "The Melancholic Delight in Male Derrieres in Basque Painting of the Early Twentieth Century".'

You're consulting Wikipedia with your mobile. With my mobile (you don't have one, but you take mine away all the time).

'Look. You'll like this. Did you know that Valentín de Zubiaurre got married (to a woman) at seventy-three?'

'Poor man.'

'It says nothing about Ramón. Whether he married or not.'

We go for lunch to a new restaurant that's opened in the kasko, an enormous place with low prices, like the kind of ultra-modern franchises that triumphed in Madrid a few years ago, with vaguely oriental waiters dressed in black wearing earphones and microphones. We don't like it at all. When we leave it's still raining a bit, the famous txirimiri. And I remember Blas de Otero, of course—how could I not when you've already anticipated I would, if you've already warned me? And I recite to myself some of his verses that I've turned into litanies (ones I know by heart and I'm not sure why): *Llueve en Bilbao y llueve, llueve, llueve livianamente, emborronando el aire, las oscuras fachadas y las débiles lomas de Archanda, mansamente llueve sobre mi infancia colegial e inerme.**

We've stopped in front of the Arriaga to see one of those street spectacles that are so popular. Despite the rain, a circle of people has formed around the stairway forming an amphitheatre. And I continue with Blas de Otero, not paying too much attention to the puppet show: *y qué le vamos a hacer si llueve insistentemente y, debes decirlo, delicadamente.**

In any event, it seems like the day begins to open: a slight luminosity, perhaps an air that arrives from the sea and pushes the clouds, perhaps because it's August, after all, and even Bilbao is sometimes ashamed of being so dark and wet (although it's no longer as dark as it was, that's the truth).

We catch the metro; we've decided to go for a walk in Plentzia, at the end of the line, at the end of everything. The metro line follows the old train track. But I continued with Blas de Otero: *como aquella mañana de tus trece años en Barambio cuando no te atreviste a decirle a Charito que la querías.**

That happens, no? That happens to them, that they don't dare, like the poet. That they continue like at thirteen. That they don't dare to say they love one another.

I'm seated in the train, half-asleep, I always sleep a bit after eating, even with my eyes open. The journey is long, over half an hour, and the incline of the tracks makes it seem like the nearby buildings rise twisted towards the sky, that they move like Proust's bell towers. Proust: you had already anticipated it. *Ahora sí que llueve en Bilbao, es el siete de agosto y llueve como en mi infancia,** Otero says, even if today is August the 20th. I keep thinking of Edorta and Koldo, of the rain, of the daring, and the train plunges into the Basque coast heading towards the Plentzia ría. *Pero llueve y aquello y tantas vicisitudes más que fueron descendiendo sobre tu vida como una mansa lluvia, ya no tienen remedio, ni dios lo remedia igual que aquella mañana en que no te decidiste del todo.**

I didn't know that section: I had to look it up in Google. How great Blas de Otero was, I tell myself, and I fall asleep almost when we arrive, as always happens to me. *Ya no tienen remedio.*

Igual que aquella mañana en que no te decidiste del todo.

We emerge from the train station and cross the ría towards the centre of the town, but instead of delving inside it, we walk along the path flanked by banana trees that runs parallel to the ría towards the beaches. It has stopped raining despite Blas de Otero, and I feel a tremendous urge to dive into the water. At the enormous beach, in the area closest to the town, I take off my clothes and go swimming. You remain seated on the sand completely alone. From the sea, I look at you and at the same time contemplate (drunk on the wine with gaseosa from lunch) the black and grey clouds that pass by quickly. *Ah este Bilbao puñetero que si no fuese porque llueve nos ahogaríamos todos de aburrimiento.**

'At least if I manage to get someone to read Otero, I'll be content with that.'

'Or to read Proust.'

'That is more difficult. I've been trying that for a long time and I don't know if I've convinced anyone.'

I Don't Suppose I'll Get a Second Chance

(Another Sunny Day, Sarah Records 060, 1992)

> *If only to myself I hadn't lied but I*
> *I threw away my one romance*
> *now I don't suppose I'll get a second chance*

The worst thing of all is the light of summer when one is nine-teen, perhaps the best period of my life. Of our life, if we can call ours something that isn't that afternoon in Holland Park, about which I'll talk about later, about which I don't know if I've already said anything. A summer. We were already both studying: you law, me telecommunications. We'd finished the first year without suspending a single subject and had before us a few months (almost three) to enjoy our youth: excursions by bike with our slickers if the weather was lousy, entire days at the beach if the sun was out, very often you and I on our own. Itziar worked and Carmen, the girl from the Canary Islands you were going out with then, had gone back home now that classes were over. You'd met her at the university and never knew how to explain to me what a woman from the Canary Islands was doing in Bilbao studying law. She was dark and strong, funny, with a spectacular feline beauty. Itziar, my Itziar, was pale and fragile. In summer she helped her parents at the shoe shop in the Casco Viejo and I saw little of her, she finished late and exhausted. So there we were always alone, you and I. You two are like a couple, Carmen said.

That was the summer when we went to buy some of those alpargatas with canvas fabric and grass soles from Itziar's parents' shoe shop. I got black ones and you blue. Now when I close my eyes, now that we almost never see one another, the first thing I see are your tanned legs covered in hair wearing those blue fabric alpargatas. We called each other in the morning, they've told me it will be a good day, better in the afternoon, there's a galerna wind coming in, today it won't clear up all day long, that in Castro it's sunny, that they didn't know what it would be like, let's risk going to the beach and if it rains we'll take a hike, let's go by bike out to San Juan de Gaztelugatxe, out to Güeñes, we'll catch the bus and have lunch in Lekeitio, let's go out to the suspension bridge and take a walk through Santurce (back then I was giving maths lessons to a kid in Santurce and crossed the Portugalete Suspension Bridge almost every day), or let's go walk out to the old port of Algorta and we'll sit in the little plaza and have some beers, and if the weather improves, we'll go down to the beach, and if it doesn't, we can keep walking out to Punta Galea, or let's go to the fiestas of Barakaldo that are starting today, or let's stay at your house listening to Radio 3.

Brief moments of frozen beauty that still ache in memory, like old photos in the family album, when we decide that this precise moment, this present of which we're fully aware (how few times are we conscious of the present!) is like a piece of recovered paradise, a pearl of happiness that deserves to be treasured: your hair backlit, how your black lashes flutter like butterflies, watching you run towards the sea splashing like a madman and wetting everyone, when you dove headfirst into the enormous wave—already turned to foam—which sweeps the beach of Barinatxe, the droplets of sweat that slide across your chest and lose themselves in your navel, how they gather the sun, those droplets of sweat, a Coca Cola at four in the afternoon, with ice and lemon in a glass, one night you put your hand on my shoulder for more than an hour and a half, the sensation your hand evoked on my shoulder, the heat of your hand on my shoulder, the warmth, the serenity, how happy it made me, seeing you pedal on your bike towards Las Encartaciones along a shadowed highway full of curves and trees, sitting next to you on the ground resting our backs against the wall of a txosna that thumps furiously to the rhythm of Kortatu, surrounded by drunks pissing and garbage, smoking a joint together at five in the morning and, dying of hunger, going to search for a bocadillo de txistorra, a Mikel Laboa concert, again on the beach, a cloudy day, but with little wind, you sleeping on the towel hungover and I reading Asimov, but I can't get past the second page because I only want to read you, read your body, an afternoon at the Hospital of Cruces when I went to visit you because you'd been admitted (gastroenteritis, nothing serious, but they left you on an IV drip for a few days) and I brought you oranges (and the doctors yelled at me for doing that), and we spent a while listening to the Smiths until your aunt and your brothers came, and I went down to the bar with them and had a café con leche and we spoke about you, a walk from the suspension bridge until we got tired, talking of London, of how we wanted to go to London, of how and when we'd do it, of what we'd do in London, watching the ships that left the port, some (surely) heading for Portsmouth, only water between Bilbao and England, shall we swim there? you asked, one night drunk in a scummy bar in Zorrotza when you started to cry talking about your mother, about your poor widowed mother working from eight to five in a mattress factory, of your poor dead mother, of your poor mother who never, ever had time to go to the hairdresser, only when dead did she have her hair and make-up done, I only saw her pretty in her coffin, you said that and wept, a walk through the Port of Bermeo, with La Gaviota in the background, saying that we'd like to be there, on an oil rig in the middle of the sea with the waves beating the metal legs that sunk towards the depths, watching the iridescent reflection of the tuna fish from above, the Cantabrian coast so lovely, so near and so far from there, another afternoon in a meadow in Artxanda with Carmen and Itziar, white wine, cava and then a bottle of vodka drunk neat, and night fell and we wound up having sex by the light of the moon (although you said that the girls were the ones who had fucked us, and I think you were right), a birthday of Carmen's, or a saint's day, I don't remember, at the casetas of the Feria of Baracaldo, shooting rifles to try and win some frumpy stuffed animal, riding the octopus, the Ferris wheel, even the merry-go-round, your face on the merry-go-round, your look of happiness of that summer, your blue sailcloth shoes and your hairy legs, the crystalline light of a little beach in Santander with these little fish that seemed to flitter among the rocks, as if instead of water it were air, a sweater with white and blue stripes and a V-neck that your aunt bought you, you looked like a sailor, not a real sailor but one of those that appear in the theatre or in Picasso paintings, in the drawings of Jean Cocteau, an excursion by bicycle from Algorta until Larrabasterra when you fell and hurt your knee and I cleaned the wound for you with my T-shirt dipped in the water of a fountain and I blew on it, and you laughed. One afternoon during the fiestas of Bilbao with the long-sleeved white shirt you'd put on in case it cooled off, and it was very hot and you asked me to roll your sleeves for you, that you didn't know how, only your mother did, and I did what I could, and the first turned out more or less okay but the second . . . the second one turned out awful. And you wanted me to try and roll it once more, but it was impossible already, I was afraid of hurting you, of cutting off your blood. And I guess you noticed the caress of my fingers on your skin, as I noticed the caress of your skin on my fingers, so handsome that summer night as you would probably never again be, and I felt the privilege of being at your side, feeling the jealous gazes of everyone, as if only for being with you caused a golden halo to float above my head.

I felt like that afternoon I had forever lost the chance to tell you something, something that I didn't know what it was, something that I feared was what I didn't want, something that I imagined would be misinterpreted by you. And I feared losing you forever. I was a coward, an inexpert, I lacked the words. I told you with my eyes, but you didn't know how to see it, or if you saw it, you acted as if you hadn't seen it, or perhaps you returned it with your eyes and I was the one who didn't know how to see it, or perhaps you didn't return it because you didn't feel the same way, but I think that no, it was all my fault, because of my cowardice, my inexperience, because I didn't find the words.

A long time earlier we had copied out in class a text, and I cut it out and stuck it on the wall of my bedroom, with my handwriting from back then, as different from the handwriting I used now as I myself was different. *Pero llueve y aquello y tantas vicisitudes más que fueron descendiendo sobre tu vida como una mansa lluvia, ya no tienen remedio, ni dios lo remedia igual que aquella mañana en que no te decidiste del todo.*

You drank beer and laughed and grabbed my arm and you were so close, so close, that I felt like hugging you like that time in your doorway, feeling the painful loss ahead of time, anticipating the melancholy of the few afternoons we had left, of the few afternoons we had left together. But I wasn't completely decided.

I write: 'Today I have a rose stuck in my throat, an arrow of unforeseeable flame that struggles to appear from my mouth in breathing the thick morning air. But today I can't. Because there are no marble solitudes within my soul. Because I don't feel the weight of the repeated days nor the slow flow of the water and of the sand. Because no one asks me to sing their pain, nor their love, nor their death. Today I have a minotaur lost in my entrails, running like crazy, dragging a heavy torch, beating and burning. But today I can't. Because there are no clay children who look at me with eyes of defeat, nor mutilated flies, nor desolate beaches, not even the dew of the wilting roses beyond the open balcony interest me (no matter how, illuminated, they overflow with invisible sweetness). Today I have a storm of the South Seas inside my head that batters my sails violently and floods me (the waves come out of my ears). But today I can't. Because today you're present. Today I can only speak of the sun.'

Thursday, 21 August 2014.
Beach. Alubias. Getxo

The day doesn't dawn too clear, but we decide to go to the beach, to Barinatxe, like always. We usually go by bus until the hospital of Basurto and there catch the metro out to Larrabasterra, but I don't know if I've already said that. When you write a novel you've got many things in your head and you don't distinguish between what you've actually written and what you've only imagined that you're writing. That's why I sometimes repeat things, and why other times I fall short and I spend my life explaining things and justifying myself.

Afterwards we walk to the beach, like always now. Sometimes, when we had a car, we parked far from the beach because we liked the walk. We talk a lot, we've talked a lot on these strolls from the metro to the beach and from the beach to the metro.

'Do you know what a *bromance* is?'

'It sounds horrible, but I've heard you talk about it before.'

'It's two words joined together: brother and romance.'

'You already wrote a book about that.'

'No, not at all, that didn't come to be a bromance, that was (perhaps) nothing. Look at what Wikipedia says: "A bromance is a very close and non-sexual relationship between two or more men."'

'Non-sexual? I don't know, I don't understand why the difference between a bromance and regular homosexual love throughout history has to be based on sex.'

'You've hit the nail on the head, I like that and I think that. The only difference is sex. Does that mean it becomes homosexual love if there is sex only once? Twice?'

'You're losing me.'

'What if those once or twice were under the influence of alcohol, or under exceptional circumstances (jail, military service, war, shipwrecked on a desert island)?'

'Every hole is a trench in war.'

'As I was saying. Doesn't it have more to do with how those people think about themselves, about what they are? Doesn't it have to do deep down with identity? With the comfort or discomfort of taking on collective identities—with identities that (what's more) are prefabricated, are given to us?'

'There you go, like always. But let me get back to the basics: do they want to fuck one another or not? Do they desire one another sexually or not?'

'Of course not, that's the first thing I told you, it's the premise of the novel!'

'But they love one another.'

'To the extreme, as Saint John said. But they live in a world that doesn't understand their love. What's more: that world isn't even capable of calling what they have love. And not even they are able to call it that. We'll see. What I'm getting at is, what I'm trying to understand is, why is sex such a determining thing? Sticking it in, sucking, caressing, moving, thrusting, pulling out?'

'Sex is overvalued, I've often heard you say that.'

'Sex is fine, it's a physiological need (in my case), like eating or drinking, and it's a pleasure (like eating or drinking). But there are people who eat without enthusiasm and drink from need.'

'Poor souls.'

'Do you know what alexithymia is?'

'No idea.'

'Let me quote Wikipedia again: "Alexithymia is a personality trait characterized by the subclinical inability to identify and describe emotions experienced by oneself."'

'You know I hate that you carry your phone around and all the things you look up with it. The discussions we had before are over, those talks which were so enriching are over now. But that happens now with everything everywhere.'

'In any case, I'm not trying to relate the inability these heterosexual men have in general to explain their feelings with alexithymia, which after all is a disorder. Because they are capable of identifying and describing what's bad, what's tragic—what's truly frightening is that they don't do so. They swallow it: those are the rules, the conventionalisms, the

stereotypes of their gender. All that stops them. It is not patho-
logical, it's cultural. I'd dare to say that they suffer (we suffer)
from cultural alexithymia. Let me continue with what the
Wikipedia entry for bromance says in Spanish: "Friendship
between men is often based primarily on shared activities. This
can include videogames, playing musical instruments, shopping, smoking, talking around the campfire, watching movies,
fishing, camping and other sports activities, going to the gym,
social drinking . . ."'

'Or jerking off together.'

'But always thinking about or watching porno with girls
in it. And each with his own girl.'

'Of course. *Mariconadas las justas*.'*

'Although Koldo and Edorta lend each other a hand when
they're young. But then they stop, of course.'

'If they lent each other a hand they were faggots.'

'See? That's what I'm getting at. They were what they were
and they wanted what they wanted. But giving each other a
helping hand in an almost childish jerk-off session turns them
into faggots for you.'

'For me and for 95 per cent of those who read the novel.
The other 5 per cent will be faggots who are still in the closet.'

'It's very helpful—all this you're saying today, this dialogue is helping me a lot, I assure you.'

'To convince you that Koldo and Edorta were gay?'

'To convince me that it's important to talk about this, that
it's necessary to talk about this, that there are people who
want to hear this talked about. That I'm not going to answer

a single question, but I am asking a lot of them, which I hope someone answers for me and explains to me.'

There are few people on the beach. We're almost alone and there's a slight breeze that forces us to keep our T-shirts on. In any case, a perfect day to read or wander along the shore. We usually settle on the left side of the beach, under the cliffs from which the hang gliders launch themselves. It's the area where straight couples and groups of gays overlap, but there are also heterosexual nudists who feel more comfortable in that environment. We don't practise nudism: I find it extremely uncomfortable with everything dangling. I've never even been able to wear shorts, nor flip-flops. I always go with shoes (if they've got laces, even better) and socks, even at the height of summer.

Around lunchtime, we return to the alubias restaurant, in Algorta. I prefer to try something new even if it's worse. You, however, love to repeat when you like a place. If it were up to you, we'd eat at that bar until Judgement Day. I guess that finding a balance between both extremes is good for us. After lunch, we go down to the sea again and take a walk through Las Arenas. That night we go to Bilbao to watch the fireworks and once they're over we go, like we do almost every year, and watch Las Fellini perform. The first time I watched them (I can't remember when), I was fascinated that they didn't want to appear like women. We were used to the drag spectacles in Madrid, where the artists take care and paint themselves as much or more than the magazine vedettes: not a single hair out of place, never any make-up badly applied, never a dress that shows what it shouldn't. All that didn't fit with Las

Fellini, who proudly showed off their beards, hair, and bellies, their make-up applied with a pancake trowel, and their tits (coloured balloons usually) almost always wound up rolling around the stage. But what I liked most was their humour about themselves, their laughter about the Basque people, something which I hadn't experienced before. And their humour about things which, in general, provoked shock or even fear. The audience for their spectacles was usually diverse, and I'm sure Koldo and Edorta would have gone to see them more than once.

'They'd be here, right? You're imagining them here.'

'You know me too well! But yes. Perhaps not in the front row, and they won't have come alone. They'd have come with their girlfriends or their wives, or as part of a gang of friends. They've watched the fireworks, have had some beers, and are just inebriated enough to allow them a greater closeness than usual. Besides, with the noise and the music they talk into one another's ear, and might even let their hands brush against one another, or a neck, there might be a few caresses, but one of those male caresses: a slap on the back, perhaps a nuggie, maybe Koldo ruffles Edorta's hair, or vice versa. They'd sit at the bar, in a corner somewhat distant from the stage, half in the dark, and they'd drink a gin-tonic or a kalimotxo. They'd laugh wholeheartedly at the bawdy humour of Las Fellini. Perhaps here, on one of those nights, is when the trip to London came up. But no, the trip to London had to be before. Perhaps in 1989, or in '92. The Fellini didn't exist then. Maybe La Otxoa. Perhaps it was in the bar of La Otxoa.'

'You love La Otxoa. It took long enough to show up.'

'I love those who are brave.'

We go back to your father's house in a train full of drunk youth, with me singing 'Liberáte' at the top of my voice.

If You Need Someone

(The Field Mice, Sarah Records 606, 1991)

if you need someone
to tell you
everything
is gonna be all right
I can do that
I can do that

The worst thing of all is the light of London, one August of 1992 (or was it in 1989), because it's always the same, the light of underground entrances and exits in which the gusts of hot air (or sometimes cold) form whirlwinds with countless bits of newspaper (I don't know if it's that way now, but then the London Underground was always full of the debris of newspapers and magazines), the fluorescent light that illuminates the face of the employee you need to show your travel pass to when you exit (never on entering), the light of some of those Soho streets at midday, which then were full of terrazas (continental style, as they call it) and which only vaguely evoked some other streets of Paris or Brussels, the light as well of Greenwich Hill, or of the canals, the steely light of the Thames, always dark and turbulent towards Vauxhall, the brilliant light of the Tooting parks, the light of the green lawn of Kensington, of Hyde Park, of St James's Park (so difficult for us to pronounce, with that traitorous 'es', so hard we couldn't make ourselves understood), or your favourite, Regent's Park, I don't really know why, although the one I really liked was Holland Park, where I wanted to go because I was obsessed with an instrumental track by the Field Mice which was called 'Holland Street', despite the fact that I didn't even know if it referred to a street in London or wherever, the light of Trafalgar Square at night when we caught the night bus back to Tooting, the light of the pond of Clapham Park, of Hampstead Heath (where the maricones hang out, you said), the light of Madrid (we decided to catch a flight from Madrid because it was much cheaper than from Bilbao), the light of that night in Madrid at a terraza near the Templo de Debod, those terrazas in Rosales which seemed so fancy to us then, the light of some mythical bars that were just the stubbed butts of something extinguished almost a decade earlier and which we visited to prove more than anything else that we hadn't missed anything: the Comité, the Templo del Gato, the Vía Láctea, the San Mateo, a long night, so much so that it was the wee hours without us even having set foot in the hotel we'd reserved in the streets behind the Puerta del Sol, and we picked up our suitcases without unpacking to catch the first bus to Barajas, so we didn't wind up falling asleep and losing the flight, although we arrived five hours ahead of time, but we'd sleep in London where we had an entire month!, the light of the blue sky above the clouds, that of Madrid from up on high, that which is reflected in the reservoir and the granite mountains, that of the dry, red land, the light of the interior of the plane, the little lights to read that you turned on and off concentrating on the Trotamundos guidebook that we had pooled our money to buy months ago, the light of a London that unsettled us at first because we didn't find anything of what we'd imagined, and in the music shops there was just Madonna, Michael Jackson, Springsteen, and kitschy summer hits, and then we realized we were as strange there in London as back in Bilbao, and we had to really hunt to find those other little shops in back alleys, in basements in Camden Town, in street markets of neighbourhoods whose names I've forgotten, or on folding tables next to the coat check of the three or four concerts we could go to (and of those we found out about through Time Out or NME, through fanzines we collected in the little shops, in the telephone cabins: you loved the advertisements for prostitutes in the telephone cabins, you collected them, I don't know if you've still got them, I do still have some, and I look at the girls and I remember you). The light of the alleys we travelled following the indications of that Trotamundos guidebook we had both underlined (you more than me, you were always more organized, there was no time to lose, we had to take advantage and see everything possible, bring everything we might need, I was much less prepared knowing that I'd enjoy equally seeing the National Gallery as wandering along the piers in search of the Globe and not finding it), of that two-storey discotheque where they played soul and which was full of astonishing black girls, of glorious black women, generously endowed and lively, women who caressed our necks, drunk or drugged, with the longest red nails and sparkling bracelets and necklaces and always the shine of saliva or tears, of black men as well, really tall men who were well dressed, imposing black men in purple or cream-coloured suits, made of velvet, of fabrics that shone beneath those lights that were synchronized with the sound and which we'd never seen before then, a discotheque that is not a disco but an apartment equipped as a disco with a ceiling so low we could touch it and the windows open onto the street, with a narrow staircase that led us to the upstairs floor in which there were just two enormous speakers, lights, and a dance floor where we danced until they kicked us out (soon after there was an accident in one of those parties, on a boat on the Thames, and more than fifty people died. We were on one of those boats, I don't know if it was the same one, maybe it was. We could have died there, of course, but we arrived there earlier, it was just a little earlier, a few weeks earlier. Surely there were never again more discotheques like that two-storey one where we spent the night or, at least, none so open nor with such easy access. Now that I look it up, the disaster of the Marchioness took place in 1989, so I can't explain how a disco like that existed three years after the disaster except that there could have been another disaster on the Thames in 1992, or that you and I would have gone to London in 1989 or that we'd have spoken of the disaster of the Marchioness precisely in that disco—narrow and dark and with no emergency exists—probably illegal, memory is always so fragile, so in our own fashion, so much that people remember having seen the Colonel Tejero coup live on TV when it's been proven that it wasn't broadcast, historians say that), a dance floor with a shining wooden polish like the skins of the black men and women that shine with sweat like noble material, and us, so white and prematurely balding, with sickly faces and what little hair we had in clumps, sweating buckets of sickly sweat, and yet those women touching us with their long nails, and they caress your sweaty curls and my forehead, and they laugh at your sweat and mine, at our haggard faces, young, with that fragile sickly youth of white Europeans, they pitied us, they laughed wildly, full of the shine of wet, red lips, reflections of saliva and drinks, and they asked us things we didn't understand, and we answered in our way and you say that they're whores and that they're going to charge us and I tell you no, that those women aren't whores, that they don't charge, but I don't know if I convince you, I don't know if I'm even sure myself, like I'm almost not sure of anything since we've arrived in London, all our certainties, our illusions, our dreams tottering, crumbling (something that wasn't bad: I in particular needed it), just as we didn't know what all those young people covered with blankets were doing in the street (begging for money? selling drugs?) because they didn't look like beggars, but instead like lords, blonde, white, with a look of princes, frozen stiff and saying incomprehensible things to us every time we passed by them, the same way we didn't understand what the uniformed women of the underground said to us (always at the exit, never the entrance), if they were angry, if they wanted us to show them our transport card, if we had to cover the photo or not cover it, with those grim, bored faces of people who repeat the same thing hundreds of time every hour, just as we didn't ever understand if one had to pay an entry fee in the discos, nor

what the cards they gave us were for and that they couldn't
be lost (or risk having to pay an exorbitant sum that we didn't
even have), nor if one had to be a member to get in, but it
turned out that being a member was free and you joined right
away (and we looked at one another and laughed and they got
upset), nor were we sure if the phone number that one of those
black women had given you after you were necking with her
for a while was a phone number or a Visa number, and we
spent a few days punching it in from different phone booths
without anyone answering until an old woman explained that
there were different prefixes depending on whether the neighbourhood was above or below the river, and she punched in
the prefix, and the number worked and the black woman
answered (a Nigerian beauty with high cheekbones and dazzling skin, twenty years old) and said that she had a lot of work
and couldn't meet us again, and we laughed and went to King's
Road to see shops, but there was an insufferable heat and we
couldn't find anything of what we'd been told, so we went to
Kensington High Street and there we did find some music and
clothes shops like those we'd dreamed of so often in Bilbao,
with Indian music we became some fans of afterwards (bhan-
gra) and in which you came to become a real expert (no longer,
now you're just an expert in changing diapers and giving bottles), a little shop on the third floor of a house with windows
onto the street and no lift, a twisted stairway with moquette
that smelled of dust, coloured fabrics with elephants made
from little bits of mirror, sticks of incense and that music—
elegant, strange, vaguely hypnotic, with techno rhythms that
you wanted to lose yourself in—and the albums stored in

cardboard boxes where, at last!, after much searching, we found singles from Sarah Records.

A bunch of names come to mind now that I remember London: Spitalfields, Whitechapel, Brick Lane, Islington, Elephant and Castle (I don't know which Infanta of Castilla had given rise over time to such a trippy name), Leicester Square, the first plaza in which we sat to devour an issue of *Time Out* to see what concerts there were that day, the markets: Portobello, Petticoat Lane (your favourite), Camden (mine).

But the worst, perhaps the worst thing of all, was the light of that afternoon in Holland Park seated on a bench near a street flanked by art galleries and antique shops in which old poofters with little dogs observed us from behind mahogany desks full of little lamps. You were looking for one of those elongated, green, glass library lamps that show up in films and which you liked so much, but they were too expensive (some years later, it was the first thing you bought with your salary as a paralegal) and I, what I wanted was to be with you in Holland Park, near Holland Street, as I listened with you to the Field Mice song so often in your room in Zorrotza, you lying on your bed, I on the floor, dreaming then of London as I dreamed of London those afternoons in your room (like now, today, I dream of those afternoons in London and in Zorrotza).

Evening fell, but August afternoons in London are eternal if there are no clouds. In the park, on a stretch of grass, families who lived nearby played football taking advantage that it was no longer so hot. Beside us, a row of bushes cast a shadow, discontinuous and gentle, upon your face. It was as if the leaves caressed your face and the golden glimmer of the sun in your eyes vibrated to thank them. That afternoon in Holland Park I knew that we'd reached as far as there, that that was happiness, that we could have remained seated eternally on a bench, that the sun would never set and that blondish boy who ran and shouted on the grass after the ball would never reach the street where the cars were parked. Then the light died, that afternoon, and the shadow of the little leaves continued caressing your face gently until it disappeared. Perhaps just a few minutes had passed, half an hour, but those minutes were at the same time eternal and fleeting, as if they contained all the minutes of the entire universe, perpetual but at the same time elusive, slippery, fulminating, but perennial (it's hard for me to explain what I want to explain, but hasn't this happened some time to everyone—a moment when life condenses, summarizes, explains—that is everything because it contains everything: the past, the future, what has happened, what is to come, but is especially pure present? Perhaps that is what I'm referring to and not something else: the sudden awareness that the present exists, that it's the only thing that exists in the end). That afternoon in Holland Park I knew that we'd reached as far as there, that this was happiness, but there wouldn't be more than that. That it was the most we could aspire to, which wasn't little (it was everything) but it wasn't much (it was nothing).

And that was perhaps the worst thing of all because, if until that epiphanic moment in Holland Park I had sensed that there was no place in this world for those like you and I, that afternoon I understood that there was and it was exactly that:

spending a summer afternoon together watching how the sun disappeared behind the one-family homes, seated on a bench near a street flanked by art galleries and antique shops in which old poofters with little dogs observed us from behind mahogany desks full of little lamps, watching how a row of bushes cast a shadow, discontinuous and gentle, upon your face as if the leaves caressed your face and the golden glimmer of the sun in your eyes vibrated to thank them and that blondish boy who ran and shouted on the grass after the ball would never reach the street where the cars were parked. But, at the same time, I foresaw that this would not happen every afternoon, that it would happen less often, that it would happen almost never. That was the tragedy of our love. Love because I didn't know another word, because I hadn't been shown one, because there were others I could have used— affection, friendship, companionship, trust, camaraderie . . . but none of them fit, none explained everything. That was the worst thing of all: I gave it a name and it was love. And for you . . . I don't know if you liked it.

I write: 'The afternoon passes between a ticktock of hours that fall wet into a puddle. I collect them and place them on the radiators to dry; I'm afraid that someday there aren't hours (not even desperate hours like those of today when I'm waiting for you). The afternoon passes and it even snows as much as I'd hoped and the snow covers the dirty greyish alleyways. And in a corner, a whirlwind of leaves and papers doesn't stop spinning. And I go down with a broom and dustpan and I start to sweep it up so as not to see it spinning so much any more, to never see it spin any more, to not have to wait for you watching it spin and spin and spin more, and the ticktock, and the hours that slip away and leave and end. You leave and come back and you leave and everything all at the same time, you sit nearby and a moment later you leave like jackrabbits on the mountain paralysed in the sun in front of the arroyo and a second later hurtling to hide away among the rocks, you slip away from me like water between my fingers and you crash against the ground and you disappear like the flame of a candle that flickers flickers flickers and goes out leaving a slight smell of blued smoke and a faint trace that disappears upward towards the ceiling and expands and unravels until it can no longer be seen.'

Friday, 22 August 2014.
Cliffs. From the Vizcaya Bridge to Sopelana

Today we've been walking along the cliffs from Algorta until Larrabasterra. It was cloudy, but somewhat hot. There were few people along the path. A dog or two that came to sniff between your legs (they never come to me, they bark at me). The ships emerge from the port and cross the ría towards open sea. The path from the Vizcaya Bridge to the old port of Algorta is one we've walked many times and feels short to us, walking alongside the sea together with other people (never too many) who move quickly ('I am going to walk'): one can tell because they carry nothing in their hands and wear comfortable shoes. Not only is it cloudy; the dawn has also come with fog. We sit on a bench along the path to take up time; we want to eat before continuing our walk, anywhere, where we can. Once past the old port we don't know of any restaurant that's along the way. I've brought El invitado amargo and you read ebooks on philosophy and political essays that you like so much. I look up from the book every time one of those enormous ships slides along the greyish surface of the sea. Some seagulls flitter above the white wake they leave behind.

After eating in a little bar in the old port, we decide to pay heed to the girl from the Tourism Office, and since it's not a beach day but a nice day for walking, we set off on the long trek (over 10 kilometres) to leave Algorta towards the old mill and out to Punta Galea, going around the golf court, until reaching La Salvaje, Barinatxe, our beach in Larrabasterra. We stop various times along the way to read for a while, to rest, although we're not tired; I, to act like I'm reading while I think about the novel. There are people practising hang gliding, others take advantage of the siesta hour to go for a run, they look happy today that they can't go to the beach and the children remain home watching a bit of TV or even taking advantage to do some work in those books that are bought in summer so the kids don't forget to read, write, add, or subtract (it's always so easy to forget everything). There are two or three enormous ships that sail slowly, majestically, entering the sea from the ría, so slowly that it seems like we overtake them walking, but it's just an optical effect (I imagine). I'd like to go down to the beach a little before returning to your house, to the house of your father, but I think we won't have time, or we'll be too tired. Perhaps I'll settle for looking at the beach from above, from the promontory that dominates it. Not knowing if a beach can really be dominated, save by the sea which can do everything.

We do long stretches of the walk in complete aloneness and absolute silence. Only a group of women shouts at another of their groups that approach too close to the edge of the cliffs (that same afternoon a woman died nearby for the same reason—landslides are common, the rock is unstable and it crumbles in layers like puff pastry). There's a man with one of those large remote-controlled aeroplanes, and it buzzes in the air as if it were a gigantic bumblebee, passes us brushing our heads (or perhaps that's just an impression) and frightens us with its speed. The man looks at us and greets us with a smile that tries to transmit trust: don't worry, I've got everything under control, it seems to say. Still, I prefer to keep walking as quickly as possible, I'm not the slightest bit amused to have that apparatus spinning circles above us. Nearby is a sign with a geological explanation I don't quite understand, at least not entirely: on the cliffs of Azkorri Beach one finds the best geological section to study rocks from the Eocene. It seems that the emergence of the Alps, the Himalayas, the appearance of the first cetaceans, the flight of birds through the sky—all of that period is reflected in the cliffs of Azkorri for those who know how to read it.

'Do you remember if you heard the Mikel Laboa song in your childhood?'

'What song?'

'"Txoria txori".'

'I remind you that it is a poem by JosAnton Artze.'

'Fine, but Koldo and Edorta don't know Artze, they just know the Laboa song. It was written here in any case. In honour of the poets.'

'The poets of the resistance.'

'The poets are always in the resistance.'

'Not all of them.'

'The good ones are. But that's not just the case with poetry. It happens in the arts in general.'

'Don't get sidetracked. Are you going to add the "Txoria txori"?'

'I plan for it to be fundamental in the novel, it almost explains everything. Or that's what I think. Here I am writing pages and pages and in five lines everything is said. Is it believable if Koldo hummed that song in the '80s, at the beginning of the '80s?'

'I don't remember. Ask Zendo.'

A few months later I asked the Basque poet (and friend) Jose Mari Zendoia. He told me many things that I'll try to transcribe here: He told me that the title is very cryptic, that the translation would be, with ellipses included, 'The bird (is) bird' or perhaps 'The bird (must be) bird' like in those cases where we swallow the verb, you can interpret it however you want, that's what Zendo told me. But don't trust whether that was what he told me or if I'm writing whatever I want to, this is a novel after all, as you know. And he also told me, come on now, let's call the spade a spade, or in this case 'the bird, bird,' he told me that. He also told me that, when it was written, the Academy of the Basque Language (Euskaltzaindia) had still not approved the unified standard list of Basque verbs and all the spelling rules and, therefore, today it would have mistakes. He also told me, more or less, that the music was recorded in 1974 when Zendo was eleven years old, it must have become famous immediately, because he knew it since he was little in the ikastola, in the colonias, where they played Mikel Laboa to wake them, at communal meals, during his first dinners with friends, on excursions to the mountain. Then they made thousands of versions. He told me that I'd need to give a copy of the novel to Laboa's widow. Nothing would please me more.

Cool Guitar Boy

(Heavenly, Sarah Records 603, 1991)

and I wish he'd see me
and I want him to love me
cos I know there's heaven, heaven in his arms

The worst thing of all is the light when I don't know what to write because I don't know what to tell, when I don't understand anything. It proves really difficult for me to explain why I love you so much. And even more to explain my way of loving you because no one understands it. If love is indeed the word. Because we've been told that one must love one's parents, one's siblings, one's partner, but this irrational love (for them), this love that two friends feel for one another—which is so strong that it keeps us from thinking of anything else—no one understands that. Perhaps it's not even love but something else. If only we were like Carlos and Joseba, who love one another and sleep together and kiss one another, who have each other beside them when they go to bed at night, who are going to get married. But us, what do we have? Scant stolen minutes, fewer and fewer every time. And nothing else: we haven't even taken a lot of photos, we have nothing to remember because our love—or whatever what we feel for one another is called (although I already gave it a name once and I probably made a mistake and I think that was the worst thing of all)—doesn't leave traces, doesn't exist, it's like a fleeting shadow, like smoke that dissipates. It's full in every moment but doesn't leave (doesn't want to leave, doesn't let us leave) memories. Doesn't let you and me dream each night of that moment when we'll see one another again (despite my doing so and then denying it). That can't be, that is not permitted. If only we were like Carlos and Joseba! If only we were insulted on the street, if only we could be like them, to argue (we've never argued, we've never had the time to do so), even to fight after a fuck and never speak to one another again. No one knows what this is because no one speaks about it. And we don't speak about it either.

I don't know if this is depression, melancholy, or just an infinite sadness. Perhaps it's not depression, but it's as if I peered into the abyss, as if I were at its edge. I'm fine and suddenly there's a light (the worst thing of all is the light), almost always a light in the afternoon (around five in summer, three in winter) pushes me to the edge of the well. It sometimes even happens that this light is not a real light, but is in a film I'm watching, or a book I'm reading, the cover of an album, it's in a photograph or a painting. It's a light that announces the afternoon is failing and that everything remains the same, that tomorrow one must return to everyday life (that light is almost always mixed with the last afternoon of holidays, with Sunday, with children who laugh, with boys who play sports). And it is the worst moment because it is the most enjoyable moment, but only for those around me: people—the whole world—seem to enjoy an afternoon of glorious light, of good weather and I, what I want is for it to be over, for it to be over already. Then my heart starts to ache and I want time to pass. It doesn't last long, the sensation lasts only a brief time, but every time it lasts a little longer. It began a few days after returning from London and it arrives without warning, without me being prepared. Like lightning. Always the light, the worst thing of all is the light. It's like at the discos when they turn off the music and turn on the lights and the cleaning crew appears and you're seated on the ground, drunk, and you see in the eyes of the woman who cleans—for her it's already Monday, for you it's still Sunday—and you know that this woman has come from a warm bed, from a bed in which she's slept with someone, with someone she loves or at least loved (surely) at some moment, and she tells you to move your feet, for you to lift your legs, that if she sweeps your feet you'll never get married (as the saying goes) and you tell her calmly to sweep them, that you'll never get married in any case, in no case, and she stares at you angrily and tells you not to talk nonsense, that you're handsome, that you're a handsome young man, that any girl would be delighted to marry you and you tell the woman, thin, her hair coming lose, with her faded blue uniform, that you'd like to meet someone like her, someone who's doing her job on a Monday at six in the morning (a Sunday night for you) and who worries about the four drunks that are still lying on the floor, who worries to not sweep their feet lest they never get married. And then she says that if you don't marry a girl you càn also marry a boy, that soon that will be possible, and you look at her alarmed, wondering what made her say that. And the light now is a white light, a factory light, and the discotheque seems like that: a factory. It's no longer a paradise of coloured lights, lasers, and people dancing, but an empty hangar with glass shards on the floor, a few lost coats, some scarves and stray gloves. Then you lift your legs so the woman can swipe her mop and you smile and think of how happy the person she shares a bed with must feel despite the fact that she wakes so early on Mondays, you think that, perhaps, to spend more time together, they go to bed at six in the afternoon, lower the blinds, turn off their phones, make love (or fuck, whatever), and fall asleep immediately after. She gets up at four and he rolls around the mussed bed, moves towards her side, the one she occupied a few seconds ago, and smells her on the sheets, and hears her in the bathroom, showering and even crooning. She is an ugly woman, skinny, her hair undone (she doesn't have time to dry her hair), but you'd give your life to have someone like her at your side. And, while you have your feet lifted, you tell her that you're raising them only because of the (scant) possibility of marrying her or of finding someone like her, or even if they were just half of her, in the future, just for the possibility of sharing a bed with someone like her even if it meant having to go to bed on Sundays when the sun was still out, and then you recognize that for your depression, your melancholy, what is surely nothing more than an infinite sadness related to the light, with the light of the afternoon, with the light of a Sunday afternoon, perhaps the best would be that: to deny it, close the blinds, go to bed early, whether or not with someone, whether or not with someone like her, or half as good as her. And she laughs and calls you a flatterer and tells you that she'd like to be with a yogurín like you, a twink, that you could be her son. She calls you a yogurín and it amuses you and you laugh and she also laughs, at the same time, you laugh together and that makes you even and comforts you. You stand up and take the broom away from her and start sweeping and she looks at you with a half-smile and thinks that you're drunk, of course, and starts to cackle now and you keep sweeping energetically and you begin to laugh as well, and the security guard comes and asks her if something's going on, and she says that no, nothing's going on, that there's no problem, that this boy doesn't cause any problems, that the guard should leave, then she grabs the broom and you embrace her, you embrace her as you've never embraced anyone, as you would've liked to embrace someone many times, sometimes, at least once, and she laughs and you weep and the broom falls to the ground and the security guard picks it up, and the disk jockey, who hasn't left yet, plays a Billie Holiday song and you start dancing with the cleaning woman, who caresses your neck and rubs your face with the back of her hand, and the security guard starts dancing with the broom, and then the disk jockey comes down and starts dancing with the security guard, who stares at him with eyes agog and throws the broom to the ground, and you want the song to last forever, but you know it will end, and then you see the security guard and the disk jockey kiss on the lips and you realize they've wanted one another for a long time, for months now, and you would kiss the cleaning woman, but you know you shouldn't do that, you know she wouldn't let you.

I don't know if this is depression, melancholy, or just an infinite sadness. I am fine and suddenly it arrives: a light (the worst thing of all is the light), almost always a light in the afternoon, and I find myself in that place where I don't want to be, from which I know it's so easy to fall, that I don't need to do anything in order to fall, that I even would like to fall, in that place where I'm defenceless, in which I'm not me (or could it be that it's the place where I am truly myself?), in which I don't want to be, but in which I need to be from time to time because it's the place from which I need an impulse in order to leave, from which I need strength. And sometimes the strength only consists of letting the afternoon pass, of not falling, of not letting myself fall. Holding on. Holding on to the pain in my chest. Breathing deeply, closing my eyes so as not to see the light, which is the worst thing of all because it's the light of Holland Park, the light of that afternoon in Holland Park on which I knew we'd arrived as far as there, that this was happiness, but there wouldn't be more than that, that it was the most we could aspire to, that it wasn't little (that it was everything), but it wasn't much (that it was nothing).

I write: 'sighing, making shadows on the wall with my hands: a wolf, an eagle, a rabbit, sighing and drawing universes of shadows on the walls, lying here in bed, in the heat of the siesta, recovering, lifting my legs towards the ceiling, half-closing my eyes, sleepy, twisting around, remembering you constantly, sighing for not being at your side, agonizing, pressing my stomach with one hand, gulping, imagining you lying here with me, getting up and lying down again because I can't stand it, because I can't bear this agony of not having you near, of having to wait two, three more days until you return, of having to endure this almost physical pain, this wrench of flame that burns me from within and twists and tears my entrails, wanting to abandon my skin and rise towards the ceiling until I explode and paint the room with my viscera until only something very tiny remains, something ethereal that continues up to the top to see you for a second, to see me dreaming you, to see me dreaming that I see you looking at me at how I dream of you seeing me looking at you.'

Saturday, 23 August 2014.
Beach. Chiringuito

'Have you heard about Kurzweil's singularity?'

'You're on to one of your odd things again?'

'They're not odd things, this is something important. Technology advances by giant leaps and suddenly (sooner than you think, than we think) it will jump ahead of the human brain, which continues to have its limitations. That day we'll have reached the singularity.'

'And? What happens then?'

'Then it would be possible to upload a complete human brain onto a computer. Immortality.'

'Immortality? What use is it to me to have your brain in a computer if I don't have you?'

'You'd have me—I am my brain. What's difficult is to upload the brain; to artificially recreate all the rest is much easier. They already do that, it's already impossible to distinguish real flesh from artificial flesh.'

'Don't drink more beer, please. Or put on your hat, you've had too much sun.'

'I'm saying that, soon—two decades at most—we'll reach the singularity, and that all of you—what you are—could be uploaded onto a computer, a laptop, and let it run for as long as necessary.'

'But aren't we something more than our brains? What about the soul? Didn't you speak to me at first, when I met you, of Gödel's theorem, of the mathematical impossibility that all the things of our brain were computable?'

'I'm amused that you of all people are the one to talk of souls. Does the soul exist? Isn't what we think we are, that depth from which we look at the world, that which is behind our eyes—there where we all feel that we are—wouldn't be just a succession of moments, a succession of presents that our senses register, and that succession of registers—which leave memories—produce in us a (false) impression of permanence, of existence, of us being something more than what we really are: a more or less long series of successive moments?'

'I'm surprised that you can say that to me, you do believe in the soul.'

'Certainly. It's just to mess about. Did you know that Kurzweil predicted that a computer would pass the Turing test around 2029? Within a few years, a computer will be indistinguishable from a human being. And a few years later, it will surpass us. And then we'll find ourselves with that problem we talked about—of your brain, or my brain, in a computer. But if one can upload a brain, one could upload all brains.

Can you imagine a superintelligence that had all the information of all brains, that related them, that moreover had the necessary software and hardware, enough to surpass those thousands of millions of brains, if it were created for that, prepared for it? Kurzweil is holding on in order to see it, I think you'll still be alive. And he was born in 1948.'

'You still haven't explained to me how this fits with Gödel.'

'I haven't explained it to you because I don't know. This is the novel of "I don't know."'

'You don't like people who say "I'm very clear about everything."'

'I don't trust them, as you well know.'

We go up to the chiringuito for a tortilla de patata sandwich. From there one can see the entire beach. The sea, shining and cobalt blue at midday, curls into waves of white foam that break in the distance and cover hundreds of metres along the beach, so flat that sometimes it's hard to reach an area where the water's waist-deep. A light breeze is blowing, the hang gliders have begun their elegant flights and sometimes they get between the sun and us, frightening us with the quick shadow of coloured fabric.

'And what do you mean to say with all this?'

'I don't know. I've already said I don't know anything, that I don't understand anything. I only know the present and that is no longer. The other day I thought about eternity, about posterity. I thought how at home we have books that will be in perfect condition, as good as on the day we bought them, on the day that one of us dies. They're bits of paper and cardboard and they'll outlive us. This very book, this novel, the day it's published, if it's published, will remain in the world, in some home, in some library, longer than you and I will. I don't know if more time overall, but yes more time than we have left. That's for sure.'

'And?'

'And nothing, just that Edorta and Koldo will outlive you and me.'

'That's why you're interposing these dialogues in the book.'

'No. You already know that these dialogues aren't between you and me. We are much more complex. It would be impossible, no matter how I tried, to make you outlive yourself with my literature, not even with literature in general even if written by someone else. Nor myself. That's why I thought of the singularity. You and I only survive if we are everything, if everything survives.'

'And Edorta and Koldo?'

'Edorta and Kolda are characters that I have created. Everything that I have invented about them is in the book. Everything that I want to be known is here. Everything of theirs survives. They survive because they are my creation, they survive complete. They survive better.'

You Should All Be Murdered
(Another Sunny Day, Sarah Records 022, 1989)

one day, when the world is set to rights
I'm going to murder all the people I don't like

The worst thing of all is the light of Barinatxe beach at sunset when I'm trying to tell you about it, trying to explain something that I don't even understand, like all those writings that are nothing more than a crude attempt at doing so, something that escapes me, like those dreams that have kept us awake all night and which evaporate as soon as we try and put them into words, give them shape, affix them to let them exist, to make them exist, but they're already leaving, they've already gone, like how smoke disappears, like the shadows of the hang gliders. Because, how can one explain something—a feeling, that which makes me myself, that which you and I are as well—if there are no words, if they haven't been invented, if any word I could use would tarnish it, would simplify it? We're on the beach this afternoon, as on so many afternoons until now, as on so few from now on, watching how the sun sets behind the Ciérvana mountains, behind the super-port.

You're lying with your eyes closed. You croon: *Hegoak ebaki banizkio.* Like that time when you told me to leave you alone. That I had no idea what it was like, being alone, that I couldn't even imagine it. Being orphaned. That I was a jerk. How disgusting. That I was a pig. That the next time I should stick my finger in my butt. And then you crouched down, you sat down on the step, you lowered your head as if you were dizzy, you grabbed your ears with your hands and began to rock back and forth and to cry slowly, almost without making a sound, and I sat down beside you and I hugged you and you put your head on my lap with your eyes closed, and I didn't listen to you and I caressed your hair and I dried your tears with my fingers, but you didn't stop crying and it rained and we both got wet and you started to sing that song that your mother sang to you, *hegoak ebaki banizkio*, the song you sing now. If they would have clipped its wings. Have you seen those little animals that wind up caught in spiderwebs, weightless, dry and transparent when only the exoskeleton remains? I refer to that: I can perhaps only explain it to you (explain it to us) up to that point, up to a fragile and transparent exoskeleton, so whiteish it seems frozen, but which evaporates with a single puff of air. But I guess that is not enough for us, it's not enough for me because we have that, we've always had that, we had that when we played football in the schoolyard, right? My Koldobika, my Clodo. When in winter (the ones from before, in your house, so cold, so wet) an ice star forms on the windows, and from just breath, with just the redness of our cheeks, with just the sparkling shine from the eyes of a boy (of you yourself, my Koldo) it shatters, it dilutes and slides down the glass, now turned into water, like a tear of a melted star . . .

You've half turned over and I'd like to caress your tan skin, the nape of your neck, like that time in a dark doorway under a really heavy rain that flooded the streets while the water flowed, dragging the trash towards the sewers, which backed up, and the cars also clogged the streets, like almost always, honking at one another under that sickly light. I speak to you now, today, of the ice star, of the little cadavers of tiny animals in spiderwebs, of smoke that evaporates, of how hard it is to explain these things, of whether there is some way of doing so. Have you seen that mark a cup sometimes leaves upon a glass table that isn't a stain but a trace of its heat or its cold, that slight misty halo that disappears in moments, in a spiral, like water disappearing down the drain, which leaves for a few seconds the still-perfect circle, almost complete, on the retina, but which no longer exists, just an idea, the idea that I have in my head, which is perfect in my head, but which I can't catch because it leaves, because it erases itself like footprints in the desert sand are erased by the night air, like those dark shadows your feet leave when you walk along the shore, the footsteps of your feet upon which I try to place my own (as perhaps I've always done, have always tried to do, like the footprints of Laetoli), but which have already disappeared no matter how I hurry, which reflect the orangish sun for fractions of a second, which are just pressure and temperature, your footprints on the sand, my Clodoveo? You softly sing:

Nerea izango zen. It would have been mine. You would have been mine. But I don't know if I want you to be mine, of course, later we'll see, your song already says it, the one your mother sang for you. Your mother: I'm going to sing the prettiest song I know, a song that tells the truth. Few verses, few lyrics, almost a haiku (I say that). You sing and the song—so sad, so beautiful, so true—sounds strange on this beach crowded with bathers who gather their belongings and start the climb up to the car park now that the sun has gone. It sounds as unreal as the damp shadow of your feet on the shore, as the heat of your body upon the sand, as the evaporation of that shadow and that heat. Like those dreams that try to seize you at dawn but aren't able to, only leaving behind the idea of something that cannot, in the world of wakefulness, be specified and therefore crumbles away. Have you seen irised reflections in soap bubbles, how they pulse, how they boil, how they twist, how they change colour and shape? How does one explain that to someone who hasn't seen it? How do you explain it to someone who's blind? How do you explain Bach's music to someone who's deaf? You can make them feel the rhythm, of course, you can draw on a piece of paper the evolution of the scales, of course, you can even show them a musical stave, of course. There are people capable of hearing music just by seeing a stave, but the tone, the texture? You can explain Monet's waterlilies to someone blind, you can even get them to touch the paint (in some reproduction, in some museum), but the relationship between the colours? The colours themselves? What is a colour for someone who doesn't see? How to explain a colour, a sustained fa note?

You turn over again now that the sun has gone and a light breeze begins to blow, almost a caress. Without opening your eyes, you reach with one hand into your sports bag, groping until you find a white T-shirt, and you put it over you like a blanket covering your belly. Always that cold—the cold you carry since you were little—stuck in your body, which attacks you even today, even on the hottest days of summer, at some moment, in the shade of some terraza, or when the sun sets, like now. Koldo: Don't you want an ice cream? You're very thoughtful . . . are you chewing some crazy idea again like always? Me: like always, of course, like always. How easy it is to not chew (my crazy ideas, I mean, not the ice cream), to be like you, aloof, distant. If that helps you to not suffer . . . but I don't think it does.

I'm going to go get an ice cream. But first I tell you what I'm thinking of. I speak to you of the foam from the waves that remains on the shore and which dissipates, of the dust of sand that rises with the slight breeze, of the final reflections of the sun on the horizon which extinguish until nothing is left, of that sailboat that disappears beyond the cape, of the white lines the planes leave on the clear sky (they're fumigating us, you say, they want to fumigate us, want to put an end to the human race, you've read that in one of those absurd magazines that are scattered around your house). Do you want an ice cream or not? Shall I bring you one? What flavour? Idiazabál cheese with quince? You swallow a gag. You know I'm just joking, since you can't stand quince. Miembrillo, you call it, instead of membrillo, and you crack up at that childish off-colour joke, member as euphemism for penis. Miembrillo is what you're gagging for, and you throw your head back in a cackle that makes two or three nearby bathers look at you. And you laugh like that time when you said I was a jerk, but then you smiled. That what I'd done was disgusting, but you smiled. That I was a pig, and you laughed. That the next time I should stick my finger in my butt, and I smiled, from how hurt I was. That I never do that to you again, and we laughed, the two of us. That you were going to beat me to a pulp, cackling. That if one of the kids from our class had seen me do it, you wept and laughed. What would happen if they saw us, weeping and laughing, both of us at the same time? By God, how disgusting, rolling on the floor, giggling. That I never touch you again, and I was already touching you, tickling you. That I never touch you ever again, and sucked my thumb and rubbed it over your lips to remove that bit of shining sugar.

I go to the chiringuito for the ice cream and when I come back you're sitting up and wearing the T-shirt, looking at the horizon, your eyes half-closed and shining. You've remembered something. About your dead father. About your dead mother. You softly sing: *Ez zuen aldegingo.* It wouldn't have escaped. That's what happens to me, that you escaped despite never having been mine. Or perhaps because of that. Me: What do we have? I say to you. I'm only capable of saying that. Me: And us, what do we have? What's left for us? Koldo: I don't understand you, I don't know what you're talking about. What do we have of what, what is left for us of what? Me: Exactly. We have nothing and nothing is left for us. Another afternoon on the beach. A beer standing at the bar of some dive on Nochebuena in the afternoon when we get out of the way so as not to be a bother at home, or because we can no longer stand our kids, or our in-laws, and we go out to close down the bars, which already have the shutters over the front door half-pulled-down, to show up as drunk as possible to the family dinner and be able to sing *look how they drink* with a smile (a false, artificial, alcoholic one) on our faces, a Sunday on our bikes, even if it's just a few times a year, from Las Encartaciones out to Güeñes at most because I've got to be back by one since my sister-in-law is coming for lunch. Some afternoon on which, taking the kids for a stroll in the area around the Guggenheim, we run into one another casually and sit down at a terraza one Sunday afternoon, and we can only be alone for two minutes at the bar ordering Fantas or Coca Colas and at the moment of paying, and we talk of how bad the weather is this summer, or if our daughter's sick, of how expensive everything is, of how bad everything is, of how bad the Athletic is doing, of how good the weather is this winter, how winter is no longer like it once was. Me, continuing after a pause: Because now nothing is like it was before. Koldo: I don't understand you, I don't know what you're talking about. I've never understood, you're always the same, you're always going on about the same things. Isn't this enough? Aren't we good now? What more do you want? Me: I want this, of course, I've always wanted it, but I want it all the time. I want what Egoitz and Pedro have. Koldo: You want us to get married? You let loose another cackle like before, brutal, raucous. Me: You're an idiot. But at least they have something, they have one another all the time. But us, what do we have? What do we have left? Koldo: I don't understand you, I don't know what you're talking about. I've never known, you're always the same, always going on about the same thing. Me: I tell you, my Koldobika, that I want your footprints in the sand to not evaporate, that when you bring your face to a window the ice star doesn't melt, that the wind doesn't blow and crumble the transparent skeletons of the tiny dead animals, that I have time to watch the circle that a cup (cold or hot) leaves upon the glass table before it disappears. That I want to say it to you, that I want to explain something that not even I myself understand, that escapes me, like those dreams that have kept us awake all night.

Nearby, a couple of boys kiss passionately, I think of Eogitz and Pedro. I think of us. You look at them and smile a half-smile. Koldo: Is that what you want, you want us to get married? You want for me to kiss you here on the beach in front of everyone so you get over this foolishness? You grab my head suddenly and bring it to your dick. Is this what you want, you want to suck my dick? You're not laughing now. Koldo: You've always been this, you've always wanted this, you're a maricón, what you've always wanted is to suck my dick. You turn to look at the horizon, your eyes half-closed and shining. You've remembered something. I leave you breathing, ten minutes, fifteen, with every moment we're more alone, but it's not night yet, in summer the light lasts a long while after the sun has set. The worst thing of all is that light because it's the same always, but you and I are no longer the same. You softly sing: *Bainan, honela ez zen gehiago txoria izango. But then, it would have ceased to be a bird.* The most beautiful part (musically speaking) of the song, the one that flies, the one that takes off, the one that rises, the dazzling ray that pierces the clouds, the one that enters through the window after a long night of nightmares, the light that comes back on after a short circuit, the water that comes out of the tap. The saddest part (poetically speaking, literally speaking), the one that makes happiness impossible, the one that denies, the one that crumbles the sandcastle, the one that despairs for its forcefulness, the one that's telling you: yes, but no, the one that destroys you forever, the one of *no future*, such a part of our no future time and we were hardly little punks at all.

The ice cream drips down your hand because you've forgotten to eat it and you remain with your eyes fixed on those ships that disappear beyond the cape. Me: But then, it would have ceased to be a bird. Koldo: What are you saying? Me: What you're singing. Koldo: That's what it says? I don't know, I sing it without thinking, I've never stopped to translate it, I've sung it since I was very little, like those carols we repeat at Christmas and whose lyrics we've never noticed, and we don't even know what some words mean. Me: I think that is the longest sentence I've heard you say in my whole life, except for that afternoon in your doorway, after your mother died, when you didn't stop talking and I only saw your lips and a bit of pinkish candy, crystal-like quartz. You laugh once more in a cackle. It seems like it's passed, that you're once more the same as always. I don't manage to clip your wings because I don't want to, of course. You would have ceased to be a bird. You would have ceased to be my Koldo, my Clodo, my Clodoveo. If I say it, I destroy you, and if I don't say it, I have to remain with this, with nothing, with you sending me some foolish meme once a week by WhatsApp, without a single extra word that indicates that you've thought of me, that you're sending it to me, instead of that, in some mechanical gesture, you've forwarded it to the three or four names that show up in your contacts, that you pass by the door of my house one day and ring the buzzer and ask if I'll come down for a glass of wine and I have my daughter sick and my wife is working afternoons and I tell you to come up, but you say no, that you don't want to bother, and I insist and say: How can you be a bother? You, my Clodo, a bother? When will we come to that? And say *agur* and I don't have any word from you for weeks, and I remain standing at the entryphone shouting *Clodo, Clodo, get up here, damnit!* and my little girl wakes up and starts to cry and I go out onto the balcony and I see you right when you turn the corner of the street (if only I hadn't seen you!), and I find out from some mutual friend, from Egoitz, that your brother, the eldest, is in jail in Toledo and you go to see him some weekend, round trip by car, without sleeping, you leave your house Friday night and come back Saturday afternoon, because you've joined a gym and you go a few times a week and you haven't told me, and you do twenty laps in the pool and I didn't even know and one day I asked you and you said that you were really into it, but that you've had to give it up, that it bored you, that you never find the time, that everything got complicated and your wife got mad and one day you don't go, and the next week you miss two days, and by the third you don't go a single day and thus the routine is broken and you stop going, but the next year, if you want, in October, or in January, we'll both join, okay,

139

Edorta?, we'll both join and that way we'll force ourselves to go, that way we'll see one another, we never see one another, joder, and I say to you: Force ourselves? Force ourselves to see one another? When did we get to this level? And you tell me, well, let's think about it, but we need to see one another more. One day you call me and tell me you've found a photo of us from when we went up to Pagasarri, it's a selfie, you tell me and you laugh, it's a selfie, we invented it ourselves, you tell me and you laugh, and I tell you that I want a copy, that I'll go to your house and take a photo of the photo, but you say, no hombre, I'll take one for you and send it to you by WhatsApp and you don't realize that I can't care less about the photo (that I also have a copy, that I keep all the photos I have with you), that what I want is to see you, that it's just the excuse, and that is the worst thing of all, that you don't realize, that you no longer realize. You don't act like you don't realize, but you truly don't realize. That is the worst thing of all, that one day someone asks me, how's Koldo, I heard he had an accident and wound up in a cervical collar, and I find out four months after the fact that you were hospitalized for two weeks with a dislocated neck, that you could have killed yourself and I hadn't heard. If I tell you I destroy you and if I don't I have to remain with this, with nothing.

You softly sing: *Eta nik . . . txoria nuen maite*. And I . . . What I loved was a bird. Me: *If I would have clipped its wings it would've been mine, it wouldn't have escaped. But thus, it'd have ceased to be a bird. And I . . . what I loved was a bird.*

That's what it says. Koldo: It says that? I never noticed. Me: You never notice anything. Koldo: I don't understand you, I don't know what you're talking about. What wings? What bird? You're like always, chewing on your crazy ideas until you lose your mind, you lose your mind, Edorta, Eduardito. You get sad and look at the horizon, perhaps you think about whether you could have clipped my wings. About whether I could've been yours even if you hadn't cut them, of how perhaps you clipped mine that afternoon in the school-yard when you told me your name was Koldo (but perhaps, in class then they called you Luis, that your father would call you Koldobika, and I, sometimes, to tease you, now call you Clodoveo), my Koldo, my Clodo, that perhaps you clipped mine on that bench in Holland Park.

Of how I would have kept being a bird even if you clipped my wings, of how perhaps I was precisely a bird the day when you clipped mine. You croon, repeating the end: *Eta nik . . . txoria nuen maite*. And I . . . what I loved was a bird.

That afternoon I thought of our world, a very small world in which we were happy with so little, four streets where we spent our childhood, two or at most three bars, and this beach: sand and water and sun. Perhaps the trip to London served for us to discover that we didn't need more than this, that outside our four streets, our bar, your car, the sand there was nothing, or there was very little, that it would take just two hours to visit all the places where my passage through this world had taken place, or almost all of them. That if everything disappeared and all that remained were our streets, our bar, our beach and you (and me, to look at you, of course, to be with you, to fight with you and roll across the sand) we wouldn't notice the difference. Once you told me that you didn't feel part of the world, that when you read the news-papers or watched the news on TV it seemed to you that everything was a fiction, that none of that existed. I began speaking to you of philosophy, but you cut me off quickly. Then I stopped talking and I thought too that maybe you were right, if only you and I existed and everything else were some absurd joke, a distraction, the entertainment of some higher being who watched us and laughed (perhaps sometimes, some afternoon, they also felt pity and repented). Couldn't they have made everything much easier? Why is it for some of us so hard to get what we want? If only we'd been shipwrecked on an island, all alone you and I. If we'd devoted ourselves to fishing, gathering coconuts, making bonfires, sunbathing, swimming on the beach until time had killed us, one before the other, or both at the same time, whatever, it's all the same, your death as my death, my death as your death (or that's what I want to think).

I write: 'I breathe sea and clouds from the horizon, I see ships that enter and leave the port and kites that crash against the sand, a dog playing with the foam of the waves that the air breaks and scatters. Climbing the hill for the last time until next year, bidding farewell to the walks along the wet sand of the shore without knowing if this time will be the final one (one can't know that). I no longer even remember the first day of summer when I came down eager to dive into the frozen green waters of this beach, with all those days ahead, with those conversations and those kisses that taste of snails, and I ran along the sand so as not to burn my feet, that first moment of pure light, of pure feeling, that first time after so many months when the first wave comes and I dive in and float face down grabbing my knees and the wave slams me and fills me with sand and algae and foam and drags me to the beach and I let the sea empty its salt upon my skin under the sun. That same sea that today is grey, that is not the same. But then, could I manage to leave if the sea were blue and shining and full of stars like that first day of summer? And what if I never learned to respond to your indecent gazes, if in my innocence I discovered that the concavities of your hands hid caresses that were not so sweet? And if when you brushed me I forgot space and the infinite rain sliding down those enormous windows on long boring November afternoons of our youth? Would I sometime perhaps regret it? Only when I see you dragging your feet head down on your way home do I blame myself for not having been brave, for not having answered you how we both perhaps deserved. There is a planet full of leafy forests, of exotic birds, and fountains of colourful water that spill over the ravines and valleys. To that planet go all the unspoken words, or those which lose themselves in the air. Wooden platforms spread above the highest sequoias, from which words scan the horizon to see if a blue sailboat approaches bringing new word, which is perhaps answers. Centuries pass there because they hope yes or no might appear someday. Shrunken, frozen at night, lying in the shade beneath the burning heat of midday, they come back to tell themselves again and again, to see if, by repeating it so often, they reach the ear of the receptor for whom they were created so long ago. But he is in another universe and doesn't hear them. The planet of the words not spoken or lost in the air is full of echoes and whispers, sometimes of shouts or howls, sometimes inaudible or unintelligible. In the corners, the whirlwinds stir the pantings and a hullabaloo of croons, songs, and complaints thunder in the ears. Other times, only after a very long walk beneath the magnolias, you find beside a little stream a shy word, enthralled, speaking to itself while looking in the mirror of the water. You understand that it was you who said it now so long ago. Or who fell silent. That's why you half turn away ashamed, regretting having been the cause of such a thankless punishment.'

Sunday, 24 August 2014.
Terraza of a bar beside the ría

You're drawing a dog on the napkin on the bar. A German shepherd.

'And your daughter?'

'She's fine. They told us it was pneumonia, they admitted her, but then it turned out not to be such a big deal.'

'Better that way. They're so little, it's a pity.'

'In any event, I'm sure that in our day when we had the same problem they didn't even pay attention to us.'

'That's how we were, ha ha. Rotten.'

'What are you having? A gin-tonic?'

'Sure. But I'll go. I'll get you another.'

I approach the bar for the gin-tonics. It's five o'clock and in a few hours we'll have to go back home. School doesn't start yet, but for us the holidays are already over and we need to get organized: to cook, wash and iron clothes . . . Koldo is tense, sad, I guess because of the girl. They've turned out sickly, every other day it seems they've something new. As soon as they go to the beach on a day that's not too warm, they get sick and spend a week with a fever of forty. And then there's Arantxa, who's about to be unemployed. How are they going to hold on with just one salary and two kids? It's hard for an unemployed forty-five-year-old woman to find a new job, especially with all her training and her experience: they won't hire her because she won't last. For 700 euros a month she won't last. I go back out with the gin-tonics. It's hot on the terraza, next to the Guggenheim, but not too bad. Even so, we've grabbed a table in the shade: Koldo and Arantxa, their two kids, and Itziar and me (we've left ours with Itziar's mother). A couple who I'm not too fond of has also sat down with us, I think she's Arantxa's sister-in-law. And he works as a teacher in Bermeo, at some high school. I only want to be with Koldo and now I can't, I never can. We do what we can anyway to isolate ourselves from their conversations and keep an intimate tone that prevents the rest of them from discretion, from butting in. We've always done this and now they've given up as impossible: you do your thing, you two keep on with your thing, which seems so important. And they laugh, they've always laughed. You're like sweethearts, Ha ha ha. Worse than sweethearts, you're like a married couple.

Along the ría wander other couples like us, some smile, others argue, and the kids chatter running around, crashing into one another, petting every dog they run into. Some young people jog with their headphones on, which makes me jealous. I don't want to say that I regret having had kids, of being with Itziar (I don't say having married her because we never did), but I miss you so much . . .

'I was looking in Google Maps what you're always going on to me about Holland Park. I don't recognize it. I don't think we were there.'

'We were there. You can say what you want. How am I not going to remember Holland Park if it's the only thing I remember, the only thing I want to remember? That afternoon the light died.'

You look at me. You don't know that I write, you don't know what I'm talking about. I repeat something which I know more or less by heart:

'The light died then, that afternoon, and the shadow of the little leaves kept caressing your face gently until it disappeared. That afternoon in Holland Park on which I knew we'd arrived as far as there, that this was happiness, but there wouldn't be more than that, that it was the most we could aspire to, that it wasn't little (that it was everything), but it wasn't much (that it was nothing)'

'You're such a fag. You've always been a little faggot. The light died? What kind of bullshit is that?'

'The worst thing of all is the light because it's the same always, but we are never the same, and then that light reminds us of the others we were before, once, those others who did things that now we wouldn't do, that we don't admit to having done. That light, as I say, always is the same, it repeats year after year, season after season, and every new nuance, every new tone, leads us to other moments whose sole nexus with who we now are is the light.'

You fall quiet. You look up into the sky. I go on:

'So perhaps, after all, the light is a consolation, being at least the same, given that we almost never ever are, and if we want to be what we were at one moment, remember what we loved at one moment, forget perhaps for an instant that which we are now and what doesn't quite please us altogether, understand why we've become this, if we are to blame or not, the light is perhaps a guide, a shepherd, a lighthouse. Being the same light always, being that light repeated, I can close my eyes now, here, now alone, now that I don't see you, that we see one another so little, now that we have nothing left.'

'We have nothing left? You're already on the same thing again? You're an imbecile.'

I fall silent now. I've become angry. You realize it. You fall silent. But just for a minute. Right away you go on:

'I switched to street view and I moved through all of it. I didn't see streets with art galleries, I didn't see the expanse of grass. I didn't see benches to sit beneath the trees.'

'You're a jerk.'

'Then I went up and down all of Holland Street in case it wasn't exactly Holland Park and you'd confused it with some other little park. There are tons of them.'

'It was Holland Park. Whenever you want we'll go back and look for it.'

'Yeah, right, I'm in a place now to go to London to go on stupid goose chases of yours.'

I fall silent. When you start like this I know it's best to leave you be. You convince yourself of the opposite of what you say without any need for me to intervene. I know that you'd really like to, that if there were something in this world that you'd really like, it'd be for us to go right now to Holland Park to look for the bench where we sat that time when I gave a name to it and it was love.

I've been thinking of writing a novel about two men who summer in Bilbao, two men around fifty, who now do all those things that you and I can no longer do, that we will never do. They go to the beach and spend the whole day there, they eat wherever they feel like it, they go for a walk if the weather's lousy, they catch buses and go from pueblo to pueblo without any hurry, without obligations. They only have each other and they're happy. They go to Bilbao to see the fireworks and return together to the same house. They wake up, have breakfast, read the paper to see what kind of day it will be. They grab a bag and stuff it with beach things and an umbrella. A sweater just in case. They change their plans every moment depending on how the day goes, how the weather goes. They wander along the beach and they talk, other times they sit on a bench and read. And they remember, they remember things about their joint life, their life together.

'What time do you start tomorrow?'

'At eight like always.'

'And are you already on winter hours?'

'There's no set schedule there, you're no newbie, Eduardito.'

'We could meet tomorrow afternoon, I'll come by your house and we'll have some wine at Aitor. To celebrate the end of the holidays.'

'I won't be able to, tomorrow is going to be horrible.'

'What about Tuesday, Wednesday?'

'We'll talk, I'll send you a WhatsApp.'

'Yeah, like always, sending me absurd nonsense.'

'You ask a lot of me, Edorta. And I can't, I can't any more. I can't give it to you. You've always asked for a lot, you've asked me for everything. And I, I can't, I can't any more.'

'*Pero llueve y aquello y tantas vicisitudes más que fueron descendiendo sobre tu vida como una mansa lluvia, ya no tienen remedio, ni dios lo remedia igual que aquella mañana en que no te decidiste del todo.*'

'That's what you believe?'

'That's what Blas Otero said in a poem. But you don't read poems. That's for homos.'

Then you cry. It's very little, just a mistiness in your eyes. You want to cry more, you want to weep so much, like that first time in your doorway. You say that you're going to buy cigarettes at the kiosk and ask me to go with you. We walk in silence and rest on the railing of the ría, looking towards the mountain. In front of us pass some traineras and a tourist ship full of Americans taking pictures. An EasyJet plane takes off behind the mountain, heading for London perhaps. For Holland Park. As far away now as it seemed to us when we watched the ships that set sail for Portsmouth one summer. Now you do cry like on that rainy afternoon in a doorway. We still don't say anything for a long while, you've lit a cigarette and pass it to me for a few puffs. Arantxa looks at us. We go back to the terraza and pretend, talking for a while more with our women and that couple we can't stand.

Your little girl starts to cough. Arantxa says you need to go, what would happen if she has a relapse, if she's going to really catch pneumonia, what a mess that would be, how last night during the fireworks there was a breeze, we'll be in such a mess. We get up. I pay.

'Let's see if we make an effort to see one another, let's join something and thereby force ourselves.'

'You're a bastard, Clodoveo.'

'I love you, too.'

'Wow! That's the first time you've said it to me.'

'See you, Edorta.'

'See you, Koldo.'

That same night you send me a WhatsApp message. You've bought two tickets to London. I owe you 150 euros.

I respond: *And I . . . what I loved was a bird.*

Sensitive

(The Field Mice, Sarah Records 018, 1989)

> *My feelings are hurt so easily*
> *that is the price that I*
> *I pay*
> *the price that I do pay*
> *to appreciate*
> *the beauty they're killing*

The best thing of all is the light of your eyes when they look at the sun. How different the world is when you live with the absolute certainty that you have someone beside you to the very end. Even thought that can't be known, given that it's impossible to know which of the two will die first. Perhaps I should say how different the world is when you live with the absolute certainty that at least one of the two will have someone at their side until the final moment. That certainty, that confidence gives you assurance and happiness in the present, despite all loves ending in separation or death, as I already said. This afternoon we return to Madrid, our holidays are over, but we feel no grief because the worst thing of all would be if we couldn't be together and that doesn't happen, won't happen, not by our will.

We take a walk towards Zorrotza, it's a splendid day, perhaps the best, the warmest since we've been here. The path is bordered by fennel plants that, with the heat and the brush of my hands, exude their dizzying scent of anise, and of blackberries that no one picks any more. Few cars pass, some groups of cyclists heading to Las Encartaciones. There's always some lost foreign tourist who's left the highway and asks for directions to the French border. There must be some sign in the wrong place, an indication somewhere that's ambiguous, because it's rather common: they travel along the highway and, suddenly, they find themselves on some back road with a few little houses that quickly plunges into the ugly and chaotic suburbs of Bilbao. We pass in front of the home of Carlota, the clairvoyant of Zubileta, who had polio and Coke-bottle glasses and you saw her at Mass, and she received at her home important people who came from all over Spain: matadors, singers, ministers. I remembered one summer when we went to see a show in Madrid and a seer (who was part of the spectacle) told you that your girlfriend would have back problems in the future. (I fell apart laughing: you were chubby then, when I met you. Then you wound up half the size and I liked you both ways.)

I remember, without knowing why, a walk with you on the outskirts of Rome. The sun spewed fire, but there were olive trees bordering the sandy passage and we sat beneath the shade of one of them. Gentle bluish hills rose into the distance and the wheat stained with poppies swayed. We were already near the catacombs. I'm sure they spread through the subsoil of those hills. Passageways and stairways and the dead in the walls and the roof. But a breeze was blowing and we'd drunk some wine at lunch and were young. And a trip by ship to Mykonos. The ship, crowded with bathers, quietly edges the shoreline of the island, stopping at beaches, and some passengers leap joyfully into the blue water (the ship doesn't approach the shore lest it runs aground). We sat in the prow and the white foam, broken off from the sea by the gentle breeze that blew above that sheltered part of the island, safe from the meltemi, filled our lips with salt and sand. A sailor shouted the names of the beaches: Platis Gialos! Agari! Elia! On the sea floor, through the shadows of the waves, you thought you saw an amphora. And I wanted heaven to be this: a peaceful sailing from beach to beach along an infinite island feeling the brush of your knee against mine. And a storm in Malatya. The sky is a cloud of hot sand, and a calm, a tranquillity of tense waiting takes hold of the streets. A white lightning bolt splits the sky: the storm, at last, you say with relief as if you were carrying on your shoulders some heavy stone— the storm, at last, gushes of mud slide from the awnings, and the unpaved ground gurgles exhaustedly after a dry summer. People hurry to take shelter in the market, and up from the ground comes this suffocating, infernal heat, sandals and white socks stained with mud. And the sewers drown. We run to the market and beside us, from a truck full of lambs' heads, thousands of cloudy eyes watch us, impassive, from their death. The mud slides towards the low areas, tearing the lime

from the walls. Thunder. A cold wind. Now they are just droplets with a heart of sun. The car starts up with its bloody
cargo. Why does death always need to be so beautiful? And a
bazaar, also there. I let myself be carried away by the hullabaloo, unaware. Crowds of fabric and unknown perfumes cloud
me, make me desperate, make me leave myself and destroy
me. Delightedly I throw myself into cascades of myrrh, into
ponds of snow, of cloud sweat. A child wants to weigh me on
a grimy scale, another sells me the sun for three coins, a fire
swallower heats the dark side of the moon, the dusty light dis-
integrates the air, do you want to see the future?, faded
awnings accumulate trash above our heads. And a summer
day in Santimamiñe. Beneath the branches of an oak tree in
summer, beside the cave. I close my eyes and the bright-green
light of the leaves stabs me, the wind shakes the branches up
high and the brilliant sparkles of glimmering drips down from
up high and colour our arms in patches. You read, I look at
the tree. From the cave comes a distant murmur, an air that's
foul and too cold which drags itself from the steps of the
entrance like some stealthy, violent animal exhaling its fetid
breath from the depths of itself. Beneath the branches of an
oak tree in summer, the breeze tasting of seagulls blows from
the curving coastline but doesn't reach the cave populated by
souls, by paintings of horses, of hands, of suns, and of idols.
And another summer (or was it autumn?) in Chartres. I swim
in the depths of the Cathedral, bathed by the tenuous blue
light that slides down the damp columns. And it is so easy to
say that the light in Chartres is blue because the nuances of
that blue are so many that they require a new language. One

can only say that sometimes it's electric blue light, at others subaquatic light, light of a well in August, light of a blue glance, of a blue sailor like those by Cernuda, light of a blue cat, light of sea, of bay, of dark North Sea, blue of the south, blue of blue sex, of rapture, light of January sky, of February, light of the Madrid sky in April, light of August in Athens, light of iceberg blue, of blue veins, of ink, of dolphins (tonight I've dreamed of blue dolphins), blue light of blue plants, of blue sunsets in deserts bathed by blued moons, blue of stars, of night sky, blue of Venus, terrestrial blue (is Earth the Blue Planet because of Chartres?), blue lips of the drowned, of the feet of the dead, of the Virgin's mantle, blue of blue milk (in one twist one can make out the blue of the maternal nipples). And my times waiting in Calle Alenza. In that gloomy bus station I watched you leave so often among travellers with their northern clothes for those between-season moments we don't see in Madrid, with their cardigans, raincoats, and buttoned sweaters. Groups of young men laugh happily before their next trip. We not saying anything, just looking at one another, not even a hug, at most a squeeze of hands without knowing if it would be the final time. But I also saw you arrive many times: when the bus finally appeared at the end of the street and I managed to make you out (you always took the window seat), then that gloomy station was Aphrodite's temple. And my times waiting on the platform in Iglesia. I was happy on the platform of the metro, in the Iglesias stations, specifically. You were in a plastic orange chair reading a magazine, just a week before we'd met and we fell in love because we looked at one another. And there you were now after seven days of doubts reading a magazine as if you didn't know that the world had changed, that we had our whole life ahead of us, so many promises, so many expectations, everything to do, indifferent, as if you didn't know that we had finally conquered all the months of April and Sunday afternoons. I was happy on the platform of the metro where you waited for me reading a magazine in an orange plastic chair. And our first walk together along and through Larrabasterra. Walking together beside the sea. It rained (but, did it always rain?). Towards the dark pine trees along a cobbled path without knowing what I was doing here beside the sea so far from my world. Without understanding what you say, trying to take hold of this to understand you better. Knowing that you've walked through these same places thinking of the day when you would bring someone like me who comes from a place without ocean, where there are no pine forests, from a place where it never rains. And our walks through Ploumanach. A northern beach, grey and windy, narrow streets so the air doesn't whip too much, full of restaurants where the tourists drink white wine and eat mussels, you and I wandering along the coast between gigantic stones of rose granite, or along a path sheltered between the birch trees. A boy in a sweater runs after the waves barefoot, but the waves run much more: here the tides rise and fall at the speed of a galloping horse (they told us that at the Tourist Office). I approach the damp sand and take off my shoes. You sit down on a rock with that blue raincoat I fell in love with (where is it? I haven't seen it in ages . . .). The water is icy and the boy comes up to me and takes my hand. You smile and your eyes are the same colour as this sea. Now, so many years later, to be able to write this I've had to look into your eyes: I feel again the air of that so-distant day, I return to the narrow streets, the smell of fish, the cold of the damp sand and the warm caress of the boy in the sweater. And my world, our world, so tiny. A table and two chairs, a bottle of wine, bread, cheese, and a square of chocolate for dessert, a glass of cognac, the sun through the window, knowing that the sea exists even though I don't see it, and having you in my bed every night.

Sometimes I laugh that my best memories are without a doubt so utterly absurd, that a plate of cochifrito revenido brings tears to my eyes or that a sunny December afternoon drags me towards another afternoon we spent in front of the TV, on a sofa in a rented apartment smelling of chestnuts and listening to the sound of people along the main street of that forgotten pueblo. Sometimes I laugh at a dawn in that narrow bed, with a fever perhaps from so much night, while you prepare coffee in the kitchen. How absurd to think that the best moments of my life I spent looking in windows of a pedestrian street of some pueblo or in the inside (because sometimes it rained) of dark appliance shops asking the price of an iron.

Of all those afternoons spent in cafeterias under the fluorescent lights that twinkled and emitted some organic buzz, seated at a formica table that wasn't especially clean, with sticky bottles of ketchup and mustard, surrounded by señoras who smoked and coughed and laughed from time to time in dry cackles while out in the street night fell some time ago and the street lamps kindle puddles of orange juice, watching children with backpacks who push one another and mothers loaded down with shopping pass by, and an old waiter, older than the world, wiping with a dirty cloth again and again, lifting our now-empty cups to see if we'd leave. But we've wound up looking at one another without speaking, just brushing our knees and giving ourselves from time to time a kiss on the rim of the glass of water you asked for and which we share.

You were worried about being yourself in the novel, in the dialogues, and you are more you here than anywhere else. Probably, I am even more myself. In the end, as always happens to me, perhaps I've not written a novel but instead a declaration of love.

We go back to Madrid this afternoon, our holidays are over, but we feel no sorrow because the worst thing of all would be if we couldn't be together and that doesn't happen, that won't happen, not of our own volition. We've reached the ría along the area where the factories once were. Now they've built a boardwalk and some walkways to go down from Zorrotza. There are panels with information about each of the empty lots, about each of the ruins of the buildings, with black and white photos and texts that speak of what they were, of what they were making. I think of Koldo and of Edorta, of the times they came down here from the park, both looking towards the dark sky full of seagulls. I think of them, in that we could be them.

Before catching the bus back, I write: 'I look at the sea of the north in your eyes to lose myself among its greyish waves. I don't know what you're thinking about, but I enjoy when you narrow your eyes and you're drenched in memories because it's then when you abandon your gaze, attentive and sometimes inquisitive, and I can penetrate you on purpose, sitting at the edge of your white cliffs lashed by the salt, lift my gaze towards the foggy, bluish horizon, breathe your air per- · fumed with grey amber and algae and foam. What are you looking at? you say when you emerge from your absorption. The horizon, you fool, the horizon.

'I want to write these words for when you're not here, to remind myself of the afternoons seated in front of the balcony, of the walks along sand paths among wheat fields. To remember so much, all the time, to remember more than if you were here. And to wander barefoot through the house retracing your memory. For when one afternoon, when that afternoon comes that now I can't even imagine, to sit before the balcony, to look for you among the poplars and remember your tired walk and the forbidden vertigo of that first embrace.'

Bilbao, Summer of 2014–Madrid, Spring of 2015

Notes

PAGE 85. *Llueve en Bilbao y llueve* ... It rains in Bilbao and it rains, it rains, it rains lightly, smudging the air, the dark facades and the gentle hills of Archanda, it rains meekly upon my childhood, collegiate and defenceless.

PAGE 85. *y qué le vamos a hacer* ... And what are we to do if it rains insistently and, you must admit, delicately.

PAGE 86. *como aquella mañana de tus* ... Like that morning in Barambio when you're thirteen years old and didn't dare tell Charito that you loved her.]

PAGE 87. *Ahora sí que llueve en Bilbao* ... Now it does rain in Bilbao, it's August seven and raining like in my childhood.

PAGE 87. *Pero llueve y aquello y tantas* ... But it rains, and that and so many other vicissitudes that were falling upon your life like a gentle rain no longer have any remedy, not even God cures like that morning on which you didn't completely commit.

PAGE 88. *Ah este Bilbao puñetero* ... Oh, this bloody Bilbao, if it weren't for the rain we'd all drown of boredom.

PAGE 99. *Mariconadas las justas* ... None of that faggy stuff.

ALSO AVAILABLE IN **THE PRIDE LIST**

CYRIL WONG
Beachlight

KO-HUA CHEN
Decapitated Poetry
Translated from the Chinese by
Wen-chi Li and Colin Bramwell

KIM HYUN
Glory Hole
Translated from the Korean by
Suhyun J. Ahn and Archana Madhavan

MICHAŁ WITKOWSKI
Eleven-Inch
Translated from the Polish
by W. Martin

CYRIL WONG
Infinity Diary

DANISH SHEIKH
Love and Reparation
A Theatrical Response to the Section 377
Litigation in India

MU CAO
In the Face of Death We Are Equal
Translated from the Chinese by
Scott E. Myers

PAWAN DHALL
Out of Line and Offline
Queer Mobilizations in '90s Eastern India

MIREILLE BEST
Camille in October
Translated from the French by
Stephanie Schechner

FORTHCOMING IN **THE PRIDE LIST**

SUDIPTO PAL
The Story of Not Loving
Translated from the Bengali by
Arunava Sinha

OMAR YOUSSEF SOULEIMANE
The Last Syrian
Translated from the French
by Ghada Mourad

JACOB ISRAËL DE HAAN
Pathologies
The Downfall of Johan van
Vere de With
Translated from the Dutch by
Brian Doyle-Du Breuil